Winner of the Costa Book Award 2019
Chosen as one of the Guardian's best children's books of 2019
Shortlisted for the Waterstones Children's Book Prize 2020

'This book is such a light-filled, huge-hearted delight of an adventure.'
KATHERINE RUNDELL

'A beautifully evocative adventure with prowling tigers and mystical
vultures that follows a young girl's journey through the
Himalayas to find her father.'
ABI ELPHINSTONE

'This jewel of a book, suffused with colour, warmth, hope and, of course,
edge-of-your-seat adventure, is the perfect holiday read. Every school
should have a copy.'
LAUREN ST JOHN

'High stakes set against a vividly evoked setting, steeped in wild mysticism.
I was swept along by Asha's story from the first page.'
SARAH DRIVER

'An evocative debut novel . . . satisfyingly classic in feel.'
THE GUARDIAN

'. . . an exotic journey with a feel-good ending.'
THE SUNDAY TIMES

'. . . a heartfelt and mystical children's adventure story.'
THE TELEGRAPH

'. . . weaves themes of faith, friendship and greed into a vibrant adventure
with a rich seam of magic realism.'
THE BOOKSELLER

'[A] warm, comforting story . . . the final ending is as

A MESSAGE FROM CHICKEN HOUSE

I loved digging for lost treasure when I was a boy, even though I never found much! But when Xanthe follows a mysterious cat into the basement of her nani's tower block, she digs up objects which unlock hidden memories from Nani's secret past – even as Nani starts to lose her memories in real life. Xanthe discovers a story of fleeing everything to start anew . . . and finds new friends along the way. But can she bring everyone together in the end? Jasbinder Bilan brings her brilliant talent for stories of family – mixed with the spice of magic – to a very modern tale of refugees, separation and belonging. It's told with love, humour and a touch of the mystical – and I bet you'll long to dig for treasure after you read it too!

BARRY CUNNINGHAM
Publisher
Chicken House

JASBINDER BILAN

XANTHE & THE RUBY CROWN

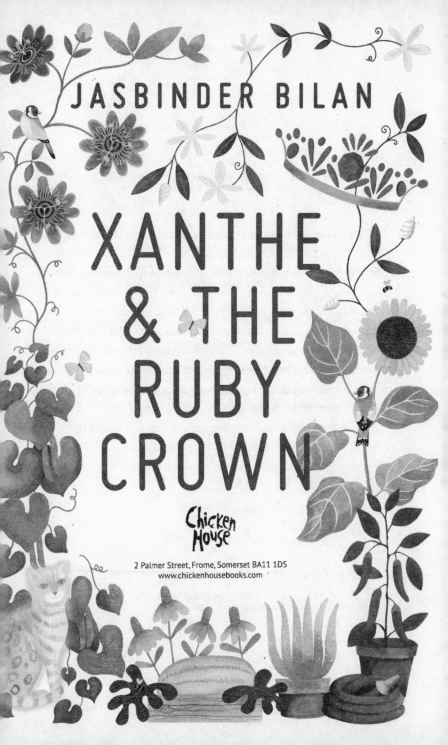

Chicken House

2 Palmer Street, Frome, Somerset BA11 1DS
www.chickenhousebooks.com

Text © Jasbinder Bilan 2023
Cover illustration © Bex Parkin 2023

First published in Great Britain in 2023
Chicken House
2 Palmer Street
Frome, Somerset BA11 1DS
United Kingdom
www.chickenhousebooks.com

Chicken House/Scholastic Ireland, 89E Lagan Road, Dublin Industrial Estate,
Glasnevin, Dublin D11 HP5F, Republic of Ireland.

Jasbinder Bilan has asserted her right under the Copyright, Designs and Patents Act
1988 to be identified as the author of this work.

Cover and interior design by Steve Wells
Cover illustration by Bex Parkin
Typeset by Dorchester Typesetting Group Ltd
Printed and bound in Great Britain by CPI Group (UK) Ltd, Croydon CR0 4YY

FSC
www.fsc.org
MIX
Paper | Supporting
responsible forestry
FSC® C171272

1 3 5 7 9 10 8 6 4 2

British Library Cataloguing in Publication data available.

PB ISBN 978-1-913322-60-1
eISBN 978-1-913696-93-1

*To all the staff and pupils
at Mellers School, Nottingham,
past, present and future.*

Also by Jasbinder Bilan

Asha & the Spirit Bird
Tamarind & the Star of Ishta
Aarti & the Blue Gods

PROLOGUE

I'm Leo the jungle cat and this is my kingdom.

Ears twitching, whiskers shimmering, I go wherever I please. Stalking tiger-like under the wide leaves in the tower-block roof garden. Sidling through the long corridors, sniffing scents of morning toast and big pots of coconut rice. I have many homes. On each floor the owners barely see me as I scoot past, quick as a mirage, stepping between their houseplants, leaving secret paw prints on their sheets.

And then down, down I prowl to the very roots of this building. Exploring every corner, I slide through half-open doors and sniff out the secrets wherever they're hiding.

Then there's something different. The sound of wheels on tarmac overhead. And a feeling, twitching through my tail.

Listen – who is that arriving?

Like a flash I'm up the stairs, up and up until I'm back on the roof, scaling the precarious high wall. I peer down.

She's here at last.

I blink and then I'm gone, vanished like the sparkle of a dream.

1

I run from the car and find the green space wedged between the tower blocks. I plonk myself down on the still-damp grass and search for Nani's flame tree right at the very top of the building in her beautiful roof garden. Even though it's only a tiny dot from here, I can see the tips of its incredible red leaves shimmering in the morning sunlight.

I lower my gaze slightly. The tower block soars into the milky blue sky and, when I squint against the sun, Nani's square windows and balcony appear on the top floor. Out of habit I count the floors and finish at fifteen. Somewhere inside, Nani will be fussing about, putting on the kettle, laying out the plates and finding my favourite biscuits – chocolate wafers.

I press my eyelids closed, enjoy the magic of the dancing light and let the sounds drift over me: kids'

3

cries from the nearby play park, the faint siren of a screeching ambulance, the whirr of traffic on the busy roads.

When I was little, Nani taught me to study things carefully. She said that behind everything there is usually a hidden story and it's up to us to discover it.

So when I listen more closely, let the city noises fade and *really* listen, like Nani trained me – that's when I hear it all, the call of the wild: the steady burst of birdsong, the scratch-scratch of insects busy under the fallen leaves and the bubbling stream that I know must be underneath me somewhere, buried deep below.

'Xanthe.' Mum's voice pings into my daydreams. I sit up, blinking against the summer sun.

She beckons me over and I walk slowly towards her, flicking a glance back to Nani's window, look for her twitching the curtain, checking to see if we're here yet, but it's too far up to tell. My stomach fills with butterflies.

'Come on, love.' Mum jangles the keys. 'Nani's going to be so excited to see you again.'

I kick at the slab of concrete tile. 'Last time we spoke on the phone, she kept getting muddled up. She kept calling me Rajan.' My eyes sting at the memory. 'Why is this happening . . . ? Nani isn't even seventy.'

Mum takes hold of my hands. 'Memory loss isn't just about age, Xanthe.' Her eyes flit to the tower block. 'Just relax and be yourself, it'll all work out.'

There's a tightness to Mum's voice, and even though she's telling *me* to relax, a deep frown has appeared between her eyebrows.

I bump my suitcase over the tiled floor of the entrance and we head towards the lifts. I remember when Mum used to pick me up to press the button, and it reminds me of being little and all the happy memories this place holds for me.

The metal doors creak-clang open and we step inside. I stare at the worn floor and crinkle my nose at the strange mix of smells in the cramped space. The lift shudders up the shaft until we're at floor fifteen, the top of the building, the top of the world.

Mum knocks first but quickly opens Nani's front door with the keys. She gives my hand a squeeze and throws the keys into her bag. 'Remember, just be yourself.'

When the door opens, I run in and wrap my arms round Nani's waist.

'Xanthe,' she says, pulling me close. 'You're here at last. I've been up for ages just waiting. I have your favourite biscuits.'

I breathe in Nani's smell – soap, cinnamon and

the perfume she always wears, Chanel No. 5, a little dab behind each ear.

Then Mum's voice reaches us from the kitchen. 'What on earth . . . ?'

I follow her voice. Mum's standing by the sink, which is piled high with dirty pots and pans. Half-finished packets of food litter the worktops, and when she opens the fridge to begin putting food away, a stench of rotting vegetables leaps out.

Two saucers of creamy milk are lined up on the counter.

'What are these for?' Mum asks as Nani comes in.

'Those are for the cat.'

Mum and I exchange a quick glance. Nani doesn't have a cat.

'What's the matter, dear?' Nani asks.

'Nothing, Mum.' But Mum's face is saying the total opposite. 'W-why don't you and Xanthe go to the sitting room? I'll sort this.' Mum begins rustling paper bags, and I take Nani's soft hand and lead her away.

Me and Nani both love history and I adore her sitting room, with all the fascinating things to look at. Like the poster from the Tutankhamun exhib-ition that hangs on one of the walls. Ancient Egypt is one of my favourite historical subjects and I wish I could have gone to that exhibition.

There are special display shelves all along one side where Nani keeps the things she discovered in her work as an archaeologist. They're only small things, nothing worth much, but to Nani these are as valuable as any of the artefacts that made it into the museums.

I love the pieces of pottery all arranged according to colour, the rocks with their imprints of tiny fossilized feet and the hefty piece of Baltic amber with an ancient butterfly caught as it rested on the branch of some long-forgotten tree.

'Come and sit here, my little historian,' says Nani, and we cuddle up close on the comfy sofa, crammed with cushions. 'What are you looking so thoughtful about?'

'Without history we'd never know who we really are, would we?'

'That's right, Xanthe.' She lets out a long breath and her face suddenly looks really tired.

'Are you OK, Nani?'

'Things just keep getting on top of me. I don't mind telling you – but don't worry your mum, she's got enough on her plate.'

'It's OK, Nani. We're here now.' I can feel my heart beating really fast, but I keep my voice calm.

'There are days when I think I'll forget my own head.'

I move closer. 'Maybe I can help you.' *There must be some way I can stop the memories from fading.*

After a while, Mum calls us into the kitchen. 'Tea?' she suggests, too cheerily. The room smells lovely and fresh now that Mum has sorted it all out.

Nani starts opening one of the cupboards. 'It *is* the chocolate wafers you like, isn't it?' she asks me.

'Yes, Nani, you always get them from the supermarket.' I give her a kiss and jump on one of the stools around the breakfast bar. 'Thank you.'

There's a whole plateful, loads of them crammed together, and suddenly I feel ravenous. I grab two and stuff them into my mouth.

Mum pours milk into a tall glass and adds spoonfuls of Nesquik. She fills Nani's mug with tea and pushes it towards her. 'Are you OK on the stool, Mum?' she asks, the frown appearing between her eyebrows again.

'Of course I am,' tuts Nani. She gives me a little wink like she usually does. 'I don't need babysitting, you know. You didn't need to come all this way.'

'I know that, Mum. We just thought it would be nice to spend the summer holidays here – didn't we, Xan?'

'Yeah,' I reply quickly. I'm not sure exactly what Mum's got planned but I can see Nani needs our help. I take another bite of wafer.

'But how will Daniel cope without you for the whole summer?'

'He'll be OK. It's a shame his architect's offices are the other side of town – but he can come over at the weekend.'

'And what about Rajan?'

'You know he's off travelling before going to uni – don't worry, Mum, we just want to spend time together, enjoy the summer.'

Nani looks at me, then. 'And you, Xanthe? You won't get bored?'

'No way – and I can't wait to see Romeo again.' Romeo lives next door and we've been friends for ever – even though we only see each other in the holidays. I really am looking forward to hanging out.

Nani relaxes slightly – looks like she's bought into Mum's half-truth.

I take a deep breath but the knot that's been sitting in my belly since we got here only tightens. It's so unlike Nani to let things get messy – but she hardly seemed to notice.

'Will you help me water the plants in the roof garden later?' asks Nani, tugging the edge of her sleeve.

'Of course. We could have dinner up there,' suggests Mum.

'And put the fairy lights on,' I add.

Mum's watching Nani like a hawk.

'How's your favourite tree?' I ask Nani, slurping the last of my drink. 'I saw it from the car park.'

She doesn't answer; a distant look clouds her eyes, like her mind has gone wandering off away from the flat to another place. 'If only you could have seen the flame trees in Uganda, Xanthe – they were like a fire, a beautiful burning fire.'

My eyes pop in surprise and Mum and I exchange a glance. Nani was born in Uganda but she hardly ever mentions it. 'I would love to see them, Nani,' I say. 'Perhaps we can go there someday, together?'

But Nani falls quiet and her thoughts seem far away.

2

Later on, once me and Mum have unpacked our bags and settled in, I find Nani by the kitchen window. Mum starts preparing supper but Nani doesn't seem to notice. The sun is starting to set, its orange light flitting across the tiled floor.

'Nani?'

It's as if she hasn't really heard me and she carries on staring out of the window, but I take her hand. I feel it shaking and try again. 'Nani?'

'Oh,' she startles. 'Xanthe . . . I didn't see you there.'

Ever since tea I've been thinking about Nani's childhood and how I know nothing about her life before she moved here. 'Earlier,' I try carefully, 'you were talking about the flame trees in Uganda.'

'That was so long ago,' she replies. 'But the strange thing is, just lately, it all feels closer than ever – they

11

were beautiful, a deep red against the bluest summer skies.' She pauses. 'But I never talk about those times.'

Although it's true that Nani never mentions Uganda, Mum's told me things, bits and pieces her dad told her. I launch in. 'You had a big house, didn't you, Nani? With a garden full of flowers and huge plants.'

She nods along. 'I wanted to go to Makerere University when I was older, to study history.' She wipes her cheeks and I realize she is crying. 'But . . .' She doesn't finish the sentence. It's like she can't bring herself to remember.

What happened to her? I didn't mean to upset Nani – I feel awful.

Mum comes to stand beside us. 'Don't be sad, Mum.' She puts an arm round Nani's shoulder. 'That was a long time ago.'

'And you've got us here to cheer you up,' I add. Seeing Nani cry tightens my throat, but I try hard to keep my voice light.

Once Nani's feeling stronger, she starts to help Mum with supper. I stay by the window, wondering what it could be that Nani can't bear to remember.

I feel something tickle my ankle, but when I look down there's nothing there. A shiver shoots along

12

my spine and I notice a shadow stretching towards Nani's study.

Could this be the cat Nani's been leaving milk out for? I don't know why, but I follow the shadow to the door where it disappears quick as a flash through the gap.

I enter the small room with its smell of ink and paper and books. There's a cosy chair in one corner and a pretty desk under the window. The walls are lined with shelves on all sides and they're filled with more of the fascinating things that Nani has collected through her work as an archaeologist.

There's no cat in sight. I frown. Maybe I was imagining things – or maybe it ran off in a different direction.

I pull a thick hard-backed book down from one of the shelves and trace the gold letters on its cover: *Early Civilizations of the Indus Valley*. I take it to the chair and open it up. The writing is tiny and all bunched together. There's a lot of information here but what I love more than anything is the idea of discovering things about how people lived in the past, all the stories of maybe a girl like me, but born hundreds of years ago in this place, the Indus Valley in India.

'Xanthe?' Nani peeps her head round the door.

'What's my little historian doing?'

'Just taking in all the stories,' I smile.

'Will you help me water the plants on the roof garden before supper? They'll be thirsty after such a warm day.'

'Sure.' I put away the book and we walk out into the hallway together.

Nani leads me up the narrow flight of stairs that opens on to the rooftop garden.

Excitement fizzes in my belly, like it does every time I come up here. Our family's been tending this garden for ever and the plants are magical and gigantic.

As we step outside, my excitement turns to shock.

'Nani!' I try not to sound disappointed, but I can't help it. The garden is so overgrown. Wild poppies, nettles and dandelions are sprouting everywhere, taking over the raised beds which are usually brimming with massive flowers and vegetables. Even the plants I know have been here for ever look brown and droopy.

But Nani doesn't seem to realize how neglected everything is. 'I'll turn on the tap,' she says. 'You get the end of the hose.'

'O-OK,' I mumble, searching under the mass of weeds until I find it.

Nani lets the water through and all at once it's squirting everywhere. I lift the hose and begin spraying the garden. All the plants are dry, their leaves parched and crisp.

When I've finished watering, we head over to the middle of the garden and find Grandpapa's bench, beside the trellis that's gone wild with purple passion flowers. It's where he used to spend all his time once he retired – I still remember him sitting here, even though he died when I was small. He loved this place. But it was Nani's papa who first started the garden with a handful of flower seeds from Uganda – including seeds of the special flame tree which sends its fiery leaves into the evening sky. A trickle of sadness fills my chest. He would be so upset to see the garden like this.

We sit side by side for a while, not speaking, listening to the sound of buzzing insects like an orchestra playing a low tune. I begin to calm down. I give Nani's hand a squeeze as a flock of green-winged parakeets flies above our heads and lands in the trees.

'Aren't they amazing?' says Nani. 'In Africa the trees were full of them. I love them so much.' And once again, her eyes are filling with tears.

'They must have followed you. Don't worry, Nani.' I can feel tears prickle at my lashes too, but try hard to blink them away. 'We'll help you get things sorted.'

'The garden *is* looking a bit dry,' she says, sighing as she gazes around. 'Maybe it's all too much for me now.'

I want to ask Nani more about how she's feeling, about why she changes so quickly. Why one minute she's the old Nani, relaxed and happy, and the next minute she's stressy, tearful and confused.

But instead, I bottle it up and change the subject. 'Nani, can I invite Romeo over for supper? I haven't had a chance to knock yet.'

'Of course you can. I saw his mum the other day, by the lift – so he knows you're coming.'

'Great! I'll go and tell Mum and help bring the things up.' I want to ask if she'll be OK while I'm gone, but I don't.

'I'll be fine, go on.'

I hurry back to the kitchen and pile plates and napkins on to the tray. 'Nani said I can ask Romeo for supper.'

'Why don't you give him a knock then and I'll take the food up. It's nearly ready.'

But I hesitate. 'Mum,' I begin. 'The garden's looking terrible. It's full of weeds and . . .'

'I know, Xanthe.' She sighs, her head bowing even

as delicious-smelling steam curls from the pots on the stove and fills the room. 'Things are worse than I thought.'

3

I close the door quietly and pause on the landing, still thinking about Mum saying everything's worse than she thought. The worry knot in my belly tightens again.

I try to breathe the knot away and focus on what's in front of me.

There are three flats on this side of the corridor; on one side of Nani's flat are Patrick and Patience who are pretty quiet and on the other, Romeo's family. Behind Romeo's door, loud jazz trumpet blasts away and I buzz the bell firmly, hoping someone will hear me.

'OK, OK.' Romeo's dad pulls the door open. He crinkles his eyes, lifts me up and swings me in the air, placing me down on the floor. 'Romeo! Your little friend's here,' he calls into the flat.

'I'm a bit old for that now, Mr Wilson,' I say, breathless.

'Oh yes,' he says, laughing. 'Way too heavy – like a sack of grain.'

I giggle and the tightness that's twisted around my stomach begins to unwind.

Romeo appears behind his dad. 'Xanthe! You're here.'

'Yeah, we arrived this morning.' We grin at each other – it's so good to see him again.

'Is that Xanthe?' Romeo's mum comes over from the kitchen, wiping her hands on her apron, Mila and Evan tugging on her dress, yummy cooking smells wafting behind her. She strokes my cheek. 'Hello, love, how are you?'

'Fine, thanks, Mrs Wilson.'

'Why don't you stay for tea?'

'Actually, I was going to ask if Romeo could join *us* for supper.'

Romeo gets his excited look. 'Can I, Mum?'

'Course, no problem. It's summer holidays now, so time to chill.' She glances at me. 'Tell your mum to come over for a cuppa.'

'I will, Mrs Wilson – thanks, Mrs Wilson.'

Romeo's dad puts his arms around Romeo's mum. 'You'll be missing your favourite,' he teases Romeo.

'Take no notice,' she says, smiling. 'I'll put some aside – you can have it for lunch tomorrow.'

Mila and Evan jump up and down. 'We wanna come.'

'Not this time,' says Romeo. 'Anyway, Mum's got ice cream for afters.'

They jump up and down even more frantically and speed back to the kitchen.

'Come on,' says Romeo. 'Let's go, before they change their minds.'

When we get back to the garden, Nani and Mum are sorting the table, and the fairy lights above it shine brightly. The sky is turning purply blue and the sun dips down to the horizon, a half-moon peeps out from between the clouds and the first of the stars forms an arc above us.

The garden doesn't look too bad in the dusky light, and reminds me of how it used to be.

A bird flashes past and lands on top of the trellis. 'Xanthe, look!' Romeo creeps a little closer. 'It's the peregrine falcon!' He lowers his voice to a whisper. 'Isn't it amazing? I've been watching it from my bedroom.'

'Wow,' I say, screwing up my eyes to get a better look. But the bird suddenly rises into the sky and I've never seen anything fly so fast. In a blink it's gone.

'I think it's nesting in the tower block opposite.'

We carry on walking between the overgrown borders.

Romeo whistles. 'What's happened here? It was always so neat and tidy, full of colourful flowers and fruit.'

We gaze out over the trellis. 'Nani's having problems.'

Romeo sighs. 'Yeah, I overheard Mum telling Dad she found her by the lift in her pyjamas. She was going to the shops.'

I grab at one of the passion flowers and tug it from the vine. The tears I've been pushing down slip across my cheeks. I held them in for Nani, but I can't seem to do it for Romeo. I wipe away the tears, as Romeo shuffles awkwardly.

'Now you're here I'm sure things will get better,' Romeo says. 'I mean . . . at the very least, I can help you bring this garden back to life.'

'Really? You'd help me do that?' Me and Romeo have known each other ever since they moved next door to Nani when we were both just toddlers, and even though we only see each other some weekends and holidays, Romeo's still one of my best friends. It feels so good to be here with him again.

'Of course. I love it up here,' he continues. 'You wouldn't think we're in the middle of Nottingham

21

even. It feels like another place.'

'Mum said some of these plants were brought over from Uganda by Nani's papa, when they moved here,' I tell him. 'Maybe that's why it feels so far from everywhere.'

'Your nani's from Uganda?' Romeo looks surprised.

I nod. 'Nani never talks about it, never has done, so I don't know anything really. But the garden was always the place Nani felt most relaxed. Maybe it's because she feels at home up here. If we can get it back to what it was, it might help.'

Below us, the streets flow like rivers between the buildings and orange street lights begin to ping on. I spot clumps of darkened trees, mysterious monsters waiting to come to life.

'It's funny how everything looks so different once the light has gone,' says Romeo. Then his belly gives a growl and we both begin to laugh.

'Shall we get some food?'

We head over to the table and Nani pulls out a couple of chairs. 'Oh, Romeo – lovely to see you again.'

Romeo gives Nani his big sunshine smile. 'Nice to see you too, Mrs B.'

'How's the family?' asks Mum.

'Yeah – good, thanks. My mum said to go over for a cup of tea whenever you want.'

Mum takes a plate and begins to pile it with rice for Romeo. 'That's nice of her, I will. Here you go – help yourself to chicken and sauces.'

I fill my plate with grilled red peppers and sweet-corn, Mum's amazing jollof chicken and rice and begin tucking in straight away.

'So what's been going on?' I ask Romeo, while Mum and Nani are busy talking to each other.

'Nothing much,' he says. 'There's a new girl called Pria. She just joined our school and lives by Wollaton Park. I told her she could hang out with us for the summer.'

'That's not nothing, is it?' I don't know why but I feel a prickle of annoyance.

'She's cool. She's really good at art, clever too – and she plays violin, bit of an all-rounder. You'll meet her soon, I guess.'

The light has suddenly vanished and the sky is turning darker, bluer, like indigo, and the warm breeze is starting to cool. I'm not sure about this new girl, Pria – unexpected feelings stab at my insides. I haven't seen Romeo since last holidays and I just wanted it to be the two of us. After everything that's happened today, I just need some normality. 'Shall

23

we ask to light the firepit?' I ask, hoping to change the mood.

'Sure,' he says, 'but not before I've had another helping!' He quickly finishes off the last of his chicken and reaches out for seconds.

Mum flashes him a big smile, fills up his plate and pushes it back – continuing to chat to Nani all the while.

'How's your school been?' Romeo asks.

'Not too bad. I'm not looking forward to secondary though. People say the teachers are really strict – not like primary.'

'Me neither, but once we're there I'm sure it'll be fine. Me and Pria are going to the same one.'

'That's nice for you.' My face crumples.

'Hey.' He loops an arm around my shoulder. We always know when the other one's not feeling quite right. 'Try not to worry about your nani,' he says softly. He's missed the fact that Pria is what's bothering me now.

Nani comes round and fills our glasses with lemon sherbet drink. It's one of her specialities – she normally makes it with lemons from her trees up here, not supermarket ones, and it's a sign that summer has arrived. But this batch doesn't taste like normal. I wonder if she forgot about the lemons this year. 'Your mum and I are going to clear up,' she says, 'but you stay longer – light the fire, if it's OK with your mum.'

Once I've reminded Mum that I've done this loads of times before and know how to stay safe around fires, she lets us get on with stacking the logs in the firepit and we soon have a warm blaze going.

'Your nani seems good tonight,' Romeo says gently. 'Do you know what's up with her? Is it . . . dementia?'

The word frightens me. I don't really know what it means, so I don't answer Romeo's question. We stare into the yellow flames, bright against the rust-red of the firepit. The wood crackles, sending amber sparks flying into the evening sky.

Eventually, I say, 'She's forgetting to do things, like keeping up with the garden and the washing-up. She sometimes seems to forget who she's talking to, and when I was calling her name earlier it was like she couldn't hear me, like her mind was somewhere else. I – I think she's losing her memories, Romeo.' Tears prickle my lashes. 'But I don't know what I can do.'

Romeo puts a hand on my arm. 'Sometimes older people have to go into homes, Xan.'

The word stabs me. 'But it wouldn't be right.

Nani's lived here, right in this flat, all her life, since she was twelve. *This* is her home!'

'It happened to one of my friends at football. His grandad . . .' Romeo's voice trails off.

'But it's not going to happen to Nani, OK?' My voice is sharp. I know Romeo didn't mean to upset me, but seeing Nani changing is hard to deal with and I don't want to think about it any more.

'Sorry,' he mumbles, sweeping his hand through his hair.

'It's OK – it's not your fault.'

'Do you think your mum's got any marshmallows? We could toast them and think about the summer – how we're going to make it the best one yet!'

I smile a little. 'Yeah, well – with everything that's going on we might need more than marshmallows.'

Once Romeo's gone, I go inside, take Mum's laptop to my room and turn it on. Going to the search bar I look up 'dementia' and read what it says. One line jumps out at me:

People's early memories can become more vivid, even though the present ones can start to fade.

I remember how Nani seemed to drift to another place earlier, when she was talking about the flame trees in Uganda. Perhaps Nani's starting to slip back into her past and that's why she's forgetting to do the everyday things like washing-up and looking after herself.

I know Romeo said people have to go into homes sometimes but this isn't just anyone – this is *my* nani, and there must be something I can do to help her.

4

That night I can't seem to fall asleep. The shock of seeing how Nani is struggling with things has hit me hard and I try to work out what we can do to make things better. But how can you mend someone's memory?

At some point I must have dozed off because I'm woken by tiny footsteps pressing lightly on the covers. I blink open an eye and in the low light I see it's a cat.

What on earth! I sit bolt upright and switch on the bedside lamp. Nani was right – there really *is* a cat! So that's what I felt and followed yesterday, into the study.

But there's something different about this cat, something special. It's not like the ones you usually see around the neighbourhood. It has long amber stripes down the length of its back and bright eyes as blue as sapphires which it uses to get my attention.

'What are you doing in here, and *how* did you get in?'

It creeps closer and begins to purr before leaping off the bed and landing by the door.

'You must belong to one of the other flats,' I mumble sleepily and follow it to the front door, where I let it out on to the landing.

I don't know what comes over me, but instead of closing the door and going back to bed I stare, transfixed by the cat. It flicks me another one of its persistent looks and runs towards the stairs. I know Mum wouldn't want me to leave the flat at night, but it's as if the cat has me under its spell. Clicking the latch behind me on the door, I follow it into the night.

Its yellow stripes glow in the dusky light as it takes me all the way down fifteen echoing flights of stairs until we arrive at the deserted ground floor.

I suddenly feel pretty silly standing in the middle of the tower block in my pyjamas. *What am I even doing here?*

But then I have a thought. Romeo said his mum had seen Nani out on the landing in her pyjamas too, so maybe she was following this cat!

In the next moment I come to my senses, and I'm

about to head back when the cat weaves itself through my legs and makes a strange purring sound that sounds more like a rattle. Then it springs down a set of stairs I've never noticed before, in the corner of the vast entrance hall.

Now this cat has got me intrigued!

I follow it down the narrow steps that spiral round and round until we're at a whole new underground level.

I give a little shiver. I'm pretty sure this must be out of bounds, but I feel a tingle spark along my spine and give myself up to the power of the cat again. I search around for it in the semi-darkness and spy the cat sitting beside one of the doors, piercing me with its huge blue eyes.

'Where are you leading me?' I ask softly. Twisting the knob, I push hard against the door but it's locked. 'Is there something important behind here?'

The cat stares up to the top of the door frame and I stand on tiptoes in case there's something up there, but I still can't reach. 'You really are weirdly persuasive,' I say, as I spot a discarded length of copper piping on the floor.

The cat begins the rattling purr it started earlier and I use the pipe to brush against the top of the frame. Magically a small key drops to the floor.

'Ta da!' I cry, smiling at the cat. 'You knew this was here, didn't you?'

The key, incredibly, slots perfectly into the lock. The cat shoots ahead of me into a large empty room about the size of Nani's sitting room and sits down, waiting for me.

There's a narrow window that runs along the top edge of the far wall, showing a long slice of pavement and street light. Otherwise, the room is dark and has a deep cavern-like feel about it but it's also warm and cosy, perhaps on account of the hefty pipes that run along the ceiling.

I think I should be scared, alone in this dark place – but I'm not.

'Why did you bring me here?' I ask the cat. But it just blinks at me, unmoving.

In the centre of the room sits a square concrete pillar that must hide all the electrics and 'gubbins', as Nani would call them. A sudden hiss followed by a loud bang makes me jump but it's only the squat boiler on the far side.

Actually, with a bit of TLC this place would make a great hideout, away from grown-ups. Tomorrow I'll bring Romeo down, see what he thinks.

'Did you lead me here to show me what an awesome hideout this would be?' I ask the cat.

The golden glow from the orange street light outside seems to sparkle the cat's fur, making it shimmer like a halo. Suddenly the cat springs from the floor and disappears behind the pillar.

Where's it gone? I step towards the boiler and peer behind but can't see it anywhere. This is really odd. The only other way out of here is through the door and that's shut.

'Cat! Where are you?' I begin to feel my heart speed up as I call into the semi-darkness.

I rub my eyes. Maybe I'm too sleepy for exploring, after all. I'm not thinking straight.

I quickly lock the door and head upstairs back to bed.

I wake the next morning groggy from lack of sleep.

It's sunny again and shafts of light spool under the curtain on to my bed. This used to be Mum's room when she was younger, but Nani had it re-done so me and Rajan could have our own space when we came to stay.

I jump from the bed and pull the curtains open. The streets are already buzzing with traffic and cars honking their horns. People below are like tiny ants milling about on the pavements. I'm still staring through the window when Nani knocks and comes in.

'Morning.' She shuffles over to the bed and sits on the crumpled duvet. 'I thought I'd bring my tea in.'

'Did you sleep OK, Nani?'

'I did, actually. I think having you here is helping me to relax.'

'Can I show you my collections?' I say, walking across to the shelf and bringing the box over to the bed.

'Yes please,' Nani says, smiling. She taught me how to store and label things properly; now, I'm starting collections just like hers. When I'm grown up, I want my house to be full of interesting things too.

'So,' I begin, 'I labelled them just like you showed me.' The box is divided into small rectangles and each space has a fossil in it with the place name and date when I found it.

'I remember that one.' Nani touches one of the labels. 'We went walking across the sands at Lyme Regis.'

'Mum was giving Dad a hard time.' I laugh. 'She was worried the cliff was going to fall on our heads!'

'But you found this beautiful fossil.' Nani stares at it carefully like she's trying to bring the memory into focus.

I take out the ammonite and put it in Nani's palm. 'Look at the way the shell makes such a perfect circle.' She traces the tip of her finger round and round. 'I had collections too, back when I was a girl in Uganda. There was so much there, so much history. I always knew I wanted to be an archaeologist.'

I'm almost afraid to, in case she stops talking, but I gently press her for details. 'What sort of things did you collect?'

'I had the most spectacular gem collection. My papa used to take me into the countryside. Kampala, the capital city, was busier than here, but up on Kololo Hill where we lived, it was peaceful and there was countryside all around.'

'Tell me more, Nani.' The light in her eyes brightens and I sense her excitement.

'There was a place we used to go panning – you know, looking for gemstones in the water. It was a river that came down from the mountain caves, carrying the stones with it, and every time I found one, I'd polish it up and put it in a case just like this.'

'How many did you find?'

'Dozens over the years, rubies mostly, all different sizes. And one day we found ten of the rarest ones. We had those professionally cut and polished.'

'There's so much treasure to be found, isn't there, Nani? Think of all the undiscovered things just waiting.'

'That's the magic of history,' she says, taking a sip of tea. 'There've been so many amazing discoveries – like Sutton Hoo—'

'The Bronze Age settlement in Suffolk,' I jump in, remembering how she told me all about it.

'I studied that when I was at Cambridge University. Or . . . I think I did, but I can't remember now.' A flash of confusion clouds Nani's eyes.

The whole time Nani was talking about Uganda she seemed more like herself. My mind begins to whirr with ideas – maybe remembering her childhood could be good for her, even though for some reason she never talks about it?

I dive in quickly with a change of subject before she gets upset. 'Remember the Roman graffiti at Hadrian's Wall Quarry?' I ask. 'It was just a few years back.'

Her eyes brighten again and I snuggle closer.

'Did I tell you about the project I did at school – about the Second World War?' I ask. 'We could choose anything at all and I decided to make mine about Noor Inayat Khan, the World War II spy, because you'd taken me to the Imperial War Museum in London. At first the others in my class wouldn't believe that someone like Noor could have been an important spy. But when I showed them the newspaper clippings, they were properly impressed.'

'That's why you have to dig down,' chips in Nani, 'and find the answers. Everyone has a hidden history behind them, unexpected events . . . like Noor Inayat Khan. She was born in . . .' Nani falters.

'Russia, Nani, it was Russia.' I try to smooth over the moment. 'And her father was related to the famous Maharaja Tipu Sultan, remember?'

Nani takes a breath. 'And her mother was American, Ora . . . ?'

'Baker – yes, Nani.'

'You're a proper little historian,' she continues. Then her eyes grow distant again. 'It broke my heart to leave all my collections. I can picture them now on the shelf in my bedroom, just like you have them, all ordered and neat, classified by size and labelled.'

'Why did you have to leave them, Nani?' I ask.

Something in Nani's face starts to crumble and I worry I've upset her again. Whatever makes her sad, it's something to do with why her family left Uganda . . . but then there are footsteps outside my bedroom door.

'There you both are!' Mum says. She's checking something on her phone and doesn't notice Nani's expression. 'I have to take Nani to a doctor's appointment and I don't want us to be late. Romeo's mum said she'd keep an eye on you.'

'The doctor's?' asks Nani.

Mum glances up, her voice smoothing when she realizes Nani's agitated. 'It's nothing to worry about, just a check-up.' I don't believe her and the strange word – *dementia* – runs through my mind again, churning up my thoughts. She glances at her watch. 'We'd better get a move on though.'

Nani gives me a half-smile. 'Good thing I'm already dressed then.'

'Actually . . . your trousers are on inside out, Mum.'

'Are they?' Nani fiddles about and checks the label.

'We'll sort it in the bedroom, shall we?' says Mum.

While they're in the bedroom, I remember the best thing about last night: discovering the new den. I rush to the bathroom, wash my face and brush my teeth, throw on jeans and a sweatshirt.

But then I remember Romeo has a new friend and might be too busy today.

Mum's already put breakfast out and I dig into the bowl of cereal, shovel a few spoonfuls of crispy cornflakes into my mouth.

I don't know why but when I think of this girl,

Pria, I start to get a bit jittery. I push the silly feelings to the back of my mind and spring from the chair. 'I'll tidy up in here,' I call to Mum, and begin stacking the plates and furiously wiping the surface.

When they're finally ready, we leave the flat together. Mum and Nani take the lift and I give Romeo's door a knock. I can hear Mila and Evan squabbling and the sound of Romeo practising piano tinkling over their voices.

I wait a few moments, listening to Romeo's playing – he's getting really good. Then I knock again, hammering louder.

'Hey!' Romeo swings the door open. 'Come in – I have to warn you though, it's chaos in here.'

Mila is chasing Evan through the flat with a toy hammer.

'Hi, Xanthe.' Romeo's mum comes through the sitting room, vacuum cleaner in one hand. 'Make yourself at home, OK? I told your mum it's never any bother having you – not like these two monsters.' She play-chases Mila and Evan with the hoover hose and they run off squealing.

'Thanks, Mrs Wilson.' I turn back to Romeo. 'I've got a surprise.'

'What?' he whispers.

'Come and see.'

5

'So what's this big surprise?' asks Romeo, slamming the front door.

'Got your attention now, haven't I! I'll show you. But first . . .' I plant my feet firmly on the tiles and get ready to sprint.

'Is it time for . . .' Romeo puts on a goofy gameshow host voice. '*The Staircase Race?*' he says.

This is our favourite game and we've been playing it for ever.

'Feeling lucky, are you?' he grins.

'Maybe.'

'Ready . . .'

'. . . set . . .' I say.

'GO!' shouts Romeo.

We run full pelt in opposite directions towards the stairwells on either end of the tower block. I crash my way through the swing doors and begin the frantic rush to be the winner. My heart speeds up, blood pumping like fury, adrenaline shooting to my legs.

I dart down the stairwell with its bright windows all the way down one side. It's way nicer than going down in the lift and the birds flitting through the sky catch my eye as dazzling light bounces off the walls.

I jump the stairs two at a time, rattle down as fast as I can, imagining how far Romeo's got, and up my pace. Once I'm in a rhythm I run faster, my trainers squeaking against the lino on each step and now that I'm gaining confidence, I almost jump a full flight. I glance at the floor number each time, smiling to myself as I inch closer to the ground floor, sure I've beaten him this time.

When I get to the bottom, I swing the doors open and rush over to the main entrance. No sign of Romeo yet. Blood pulses in my temples, heart thudding hard against my ribs.

Where is he? All I can see are the mums pushing buggies and the older neighbours on their way to the shops, people milling around the community hub, taking a minute to chat.

'Boo!' He jumps out at me and I nearly have a heart attack.

'Argh, Romeo. How did you get down first?' I say between breaths.

'More practice than you, clearly,' he smiles.

'Oh man, I was sure I was going to win.' I hold my sides, waiting for my breathing to get back to normal.

'Next time!' The sweat-beads at the edges of Romeo's hairline glisten in the morning sun. They light up his beautiful red Afro and he looks like an angel with a burning halo. He can't stop beaming.

'OK, OK! Don't rub it in.' I know he won fair and square, but I bust a gut to beat him and a small part of me is a little disappointed. 'Do you still want to see the surprise?'

I lead him back into the far corner of the building where the cat led me late last night. He follows me down the spiral staircase.

'I've never noticed this before,' he says, as he clangs down the metal steps behind me.

'Well, no one bothers to come down here, which is why it's perfect.'

'Perfect for what?'

We stand before the black metal door, the paint peeling, the torn *No Entry* sign making it look pretty uninviting in the daylight.

Romeo raises his eyebrows.

'Bear with me.' I fish for the key I found last night, which I slid right up against the wall, beside the door frame. I slot it into the lock and push the door open. 'Ta da!'

The door bangs shut behind us.

'Impressive!' Romeo says sarcastically. He bats away the tangly spiders' webs that have caught in his hair.

'It will be,' I say, ignoring him. In the daylight, it looks a bit grubby and tired. But I know this can work. 'We just need to give it a lick of paint, bring some cushions down. It'll be our own private den, away from all the grown-ups.'

'It's quite bright for a basement,' says Romeo, walking around the space. 'How did you find it?'

'I couldn't sleep last night and somehow this cat's been getting into Nani's flat. Last night it woke me up and seemed to want me to follow it. This is where it brought me.'

'Spooky.' Romeo makes ghosty arms. 'Coming here in the middle of the night . . . What did this cat look like? I might know who it belongs to.'

'It's like a mini-tiger, has sort of golden fur and these massive blue eyes.'

Romeo frowns. 'There are a few tabbies in the block, but I've never seen one with blue eyes.'

Shafts of yellow light from the high narrow window shine on the shabby walls.

'Well, what do you think?' I say. 'Shall we get it all cosy? Nani's probably got some old cushions we can have.'

'Great find, Xanthe, but we should probably start by cleaning it up.'

We rush back to the flats and return armed with a brush and a few cleaning cloths. For the first time, I notice there's a second door at the far end of the room and feel a twinge of relief. This must be how the cat disappeared last night. But when we try the door, it's bolted.

After a bit of effort we manage to open it and let some air in – but there's no way the cat slipped outside this way.

Beyond the door is a small tarmacked courtyard with a stack of pallets shoved to one side and a big metal bin next to them.

Romeo gets busy sweeping the floor and I focus on the tangly cobwebs.

'It's looking better already,' says Romeo, swinging the brush about, sending dust flying into the air.

The basement is bigger than we thought and it takes a while to get rid of all the piles of dirt.

The whole time we've been down here I haven't thought about Nani's visit to the doctor at all, but when I look at my watch, I feel my stomach churning again and wonder if they're back yet and what happened.

'I think we've done as much as we can for one day,' I say. 'Mum and Nani will be back soon, anyway.'

Romeo flops against the wall. 'Agreed – it's tiring doing housework.'

We head out into the hallway and I lock the door to the den.

'Let's leave the key here.' I slip it under the dark gap between the door and the floor. 'That way we can both get in whenever we need to.'

6

When I get back to the flat I hear Mum and Nani in the kitchen. I take off my coat and hang it on the pegs. Mum's bag is on the table and I notice there are some leaflets poking out of the top.

I wouldn't normally nose around Mum's things but the writing on one of them reads *Treetops Lodge*. Maybe Mum's planning a little mini-break for us! I can't resist and pull the leaflet out to take a closer look, but it isn't a mini-break at all. Treetops Lodge is a home for old people!

I shove the leaflet back, anger bubbling up inside. Why is Mum looking at old people's homes? Doesn't she realize what a bad idea that would be? It means everything would change – the flat Great-grandpa worked so hard for would be sold, all my visits would just become memories and I'd hardly ever see Romeo again. And Nani would end up sitting in a chair all day staring out of the window. I've seen the TV documentaries!

I dig my heels into the floor. I meant what I said about looking after Nani – there's no way I'll let this happen.

I storm into the kitchen. Mum and Nani are sitting at the table with cups of tea. I give Mum a glare but I can't say anything in front of Nani – I don't want to upset her – so I bite my tongue. *The tower block is my history too*, I want to say, *and if I lose it, it'll be like losing a whole chunk of who I am and everything that came before.*

'Hey, love, did you have a nice time round at Romeo's?'

'Yes thanks,' I blurt.

'What's wrong with you?' asks Mum, taking a sip of tea.

'I expect she's hungry,' says Nani, pulling her chair out. 'It's already past lunch. How about a toastie?'

I make my voice gentler. 'That would be yum, thanks, Nani.'

I'm trying to read Mum's face to find out what happened at the doctor's and why she's thinking of sending Nani to a home, but she's concentrating hard on the contents of her mug.

Nani gets the toastie maker out and begins to grate a carrot.

'I think you meant to get cheese, Nani.' I go to the fridge, pour myself some juice and hand her the block of Cheddar, trying to make it seem as normal as I can, but Nani's confusing everything. The news from the doctor must be bad and I'm scared. The hum of the fridge is like a too-loud insect noise, trying to cover up the fact that nobody is saying much.

I sit opposite Mum. She fiddles with an earring like she does when she's worrying over something – it seems like there's news but she's keeping it to herself. Or maybe she just doesn't want to say anything in front of Nani?

'Here you are, dear.' Nani puts the toastie and a few crisps in front of me. '*Bon appétit!*'

'*Merci*, madame!' I giggle, trying to sound normal and tucking into the melted cheese. 'Just like being on proper holiday.'

'Do you remember when we went to Paris a few years ago?' says Mum, beginning to relax.

'Didn't we go on the Eurostar?' asks Nani. 'And walk along the Champs-Élysées?'

'Ah – I loved it,' I say, taking another bite.

'I think you wanted us to move there,' laughs Mum.

'I remember the ride on the river,' says Nani. 'And

the perfume you bought me – Chanel No. 5, my favourite.'

After I've finished my toastie, Nani goes to the sitting room while Mum busies herself tidying things in the kitchen. I take Nani another cup of tea. She looks tired and I imagine she's thinking about the visit to the doctor's – just like I am, and Mum is, although none of us are talking about it. I wonder if I should ask Nani what happened, but I'm scared she'll get sad again.

'Why don't you put your feet up, Nani?' I slide the tea on to the side table.

'Thank you, Xanthe. I *am* feeling a bit tired.' Her face clouds over. 'It's so lovely having you here.'

I take her hand in mine, feel her smooth skin and remember all the times she held my hand when I was little, made me feel safe, and I make myself a promise to do the same for her.

Nani takes another sip of tea and stares out of the window.

'Why don't you show me your collections, dear?'

I bite the side of my cheek. We already looked at them but I don't know if I should say that or just go along with Nani. I decide to go along with it. 'Mmm . . . I'll go and get them now.'

When I go to my room, Mum's in there tidying

my things up.

'W . . . what did the doctor say?' Should I mention about finding the leaflets?

'I don't want you to worry,' says Mum, folding my T-shirt over and over.

'It's worse not knowing though – I can help.'

Mum frowns and stuffs the T-shirt into the drawer. 'She did a few checks, that's all, said we need to monitor Nani, but not to alarm her.' Mum takes a deep breath. 'Xanthe – the doctor said that Nani's showing early signs of dementia. But it's important to stay calm and be normal. There's some more advice but . . . I can't process everything right now. I need a few minutes. OK?'

I feel scared but I swallow, pushing the feeling deep down inside. 'OK – be normal. I can do that.'

I pick up my collections and go back to the sitting room. I put them on the coffee table in front of Nani. I tell myself to act normal. I hope she can't see I'm trying not to cry.

'Shall we sit over here to look at them?' I suggest.

Nani joins me on the sofa and I take the first box and lay it on my knee. 'These are my ammonites.'

Nani studies them. 'Yes, all in order.' She uses her finger to find the first entry. '2017,' she reads, 'Lyme Regis.'

'It was after that trip that you suggested I make my own collections.'

'Yes – that's right.' I can tell Nani is thinking about the day, testing herself to see what else she can recall. 'We had ice cream on the beach after.'

She's frowning, as if struggling to remember – but I keep on talking. 'That was my very first fossil and you helped me type the label on your old typewriter. You said it was easier than printing it all out from the computer. I labelled everything just like you showed me.'

'Oh yes! That old typewriter – whatever happened to it?'

'You gave it to me – I've got it in my room at home.'

'I remember back in Uganda when I was a little girl like you, I loved collecting things too, but of course I had to leave them behind.' She shakes her head. 'It's like those memories are getting clearer but everything else is fuzzy.'

Nani's face lights up when she talks about Uganda – I wonder again if talking about her childhood is helping. I decide to tread carefully – to ask her only about happy things.

We sit together all cosied up on the sofa. 'Can you tell me more about your jewels, Nani? The ones you

50

found in the river, back when you were a little girl like me?'

'The colours were so bright – deepest ruby reds,' she replies. Her eyes are focused, like she wants to remember all of it. 'I remember wading in the warm waters, my shorts flapping in the breeze. I was so excited by our find and I scooped the little gems up. I can see them now lying in my palm, shiny with river water.'

'And what else did you collect?'

'I had a collection of feathers too.'

'Really?' I urge, swept up by Nani's enthusiasm.

'Yes.' She smiles. 'I had so many feathers I kept them in a big box under the bed – but the special ones I put in a collection.'

'Which were your favourites?'

'I had a long grey feather from the crested crane and a brilliant blue one from a great blue turaco . . . but my favourite was probably the tiny red one I found on a school trip when we went to the forests . . . it was from a shelley's crimsonwing.'

'Shall I see if I can find one on my phone?' I type in the name and a photo of the cutest, tiniest bird pings up. I push it across to Nani.

'There it is.' She smiles the biggest smile, her eyes filling with sparkle. 'Thank you, Xanthe.'

'I can see why it was your favourite.'

'The feather was so pretty and soft as silk. I called it my lucky feather.'

'It sounds so magical, Nani. If it was me I would have stayed there for ever and ever. Why didn't you bring your collections with you?'

Nani's face changes in a heartbeat; her eyes glaze over and I realize my mistake. I was supposed to stick to happy topics – but now I've slipped up I can't help but carry on. I feel drawn to the subject like it's magnetic. I *need* to know.

'What is it?' I ask gently. 'Did something bad happen when you left?'

'No more,' she says, her lip trembling.

'I'm sorry,' I murmur, feeling terrible.

I can see that something happened in Uganda, something so bad that she doesn't want to remember – but I keep thinking about how much better she seems when she *does* remember her childhood. If I can only help her to face whatever it is that was so difficult, perhaps she'll feel better all the time.

'What are you two plotting?' Mum has slipped into the sitting room without us noticing and hovers awkwardly in the doorway.

'I – we were just talking. Nani was telling me about her collections. The ones she had as a child.'

'Are you OK, Mum?' My mum sits on the other side of Nani and studies her face. 'You know, one of the things the doctor said was to make a life story. Like a scrapbook, full of all your memories. Would you like that?'

Nani's face is back to normal; it's as if she's locked whatever she'd remembered away again. 'I don't want to remember *all* of it.'

I wonder if Mum knows what memories she's buried deep inside?

'Of course,' Mum says. 'You can remember whatever you like, one step at a time. We can use photos and pictures.'

'We could do it together, Nani!' I cry. This would be doing something rather than just worrying and I can feel a buzz of excitement, because I'll get to find out more about Nani too.

Nani squeezes my hand and smiles and I feel relief. She's not angry with me for upsetting her.

'I think Nani should have a nap,' says Mum.

'You don't have to talk like I'm not here,' replies Nani, folding her hands in her lap.

'Sorry,' Mum says, her shoulders tight. 'I didn't mean to.'

'But maybe you're right,' Nani adds. 'That doctor was talking so much it made me dizzy.'

*

Once Nani has left for her room, I take the box of ammonites back to mine. I've barely put them down when I feel something soft as a feather brush against my leg. The cat!

'How did *you* get in? And where did you disappear to last night?' It's staring at me with its deep-blue eyes. I lean towards it to give it a stroke but it slides away, flicking its tail. 'Oi. I was only going to make a fuss.'

It turns to go and I follow it back into Nani's study. The cat sidles elegantly against the bookshelves, then begins pawing at a specific section at the bottom.

'What is it? Is there something there?' I ask.

There's a carved wooden pillar set in the bookcase as decoration – the cat's tapping right at the base of it. I shuffle on my hands and knees to get a look. Last time this cat led me to the basement den . . . maybe there's something interesting here too?

'I can't see anything there,' I say.

The cat continues to claw at the plinth. I hook my fingers around the edges – there's a slight indentation and I realize it's not totally attached. When I pull the edges it slowly gives way.

I feel my breath hitch. There really *is* something hidden here!

Behind the plinth, it's dark and dusty; cobwebs cover the opening and tiny insects lie dead on the shadowy floor. But the cat's purring encouragingly, so I hold my nerve and push my hands into the space. My fingers catch on something solid and I pull it out into the light to get a better look.

'What's this?' I ask, staring at the shoebox covered in dirt and grime.

The cat sits patiently by my side as I blow years of dust into the air and wipe it down with my sleeve.

'Shall we have a look?'

I lift the lid and inside is another box, but this one is a bit smaller and much more beautiful. It looks special, like the sort you'd save for something that meant a lot. It's made from carved wood and the top is inlaid with bright pieces of pearly shell.

I swallow and dart a glance over to the door. I feel like I've stumbled on a secret – something Nani wouldn't want me to see. The cat begins that thunderous rattling purr. 'Shhh,' I warn.

My chest tightens as I lift the lid.

Inside, cushioned by tissue paper, is a pressed flower. It's bright orangey red with long petals a bit like a lily. It looks fragile and I know I probably shouldn't touch it but I can't help myself.

I take the flower gently from its box and place it in

my palm. I feel a whoosh like a breeze from an open window; it's warm and filled with the most incredible fragrance. A slight dizziness makes me swoon and I lean against the bookcase to steady myself . . .

When I open my eyes, it's like the carpet of the study has turned into grass and the pillars on the bookcases are tree trunks, rough under my fingers.

'Where . . . ?' I trail off because my voice sounds like it's underwater.

The light grows brighter, as if I'm outside. When I glance up I realize the ceiling is gone and instead there's boundless blue sky, the sun beating down on my face. As I watch, branches sprout from the trunks and cover the books in lush leaves.

Now the study has gone altogether and I'm standing in a huge garden. The cat is sitting on one of the tree's low branches, its eyes fixed on me as if challenging me to be afraid. But for some reason, I'm not.

Suddenly a little girl runs across my line of vision. She's wearing a pretty dress as if she's going to a party. She runs further into the garden, through the tall trees with swaying branches, and hides behind one of them.

The cat turns its attention away from me and stretches out, enjoying the sun.

'Maia,' a voice calls out. A young woman with her

hair wrapped in a colourful scarf chases towards the little girl. 'Where are you hiding?'

Maia lets out a squeal. 'Mercy!' she cries and jumps out from behind the tree. It's a beautiful tree with burnt-orange flowers dotting the tall branches and scattered like flames under its canopy.

The young woman bundles Maia into a hug and lifts her off the ground. She tucks a bright flower into her hair. 'There,' she says. 'So pretty.'

She takes Maia by the hand and they walk back through the garden towards the house. Maia, the little girl, stares up at the young woman and when I look into her eyes, it's clear the two of them are really close.

A long table laid with food and drink stands on the verandah. There are lots of children there and it seems like it's the little girl's birthday. A man and woman – Maia's mum and dad – are waving and telling them to hurry.

Bunting is strung above the table and there's excited clapping as Maia and Mercy return to the party. I see flashes of red and green as birds fly from one end of the garden to the other. The sky is a deeper blue and now a small thumbnail of a moon sits high between the branches of the trees.

A phone rings and the man answers it. As soon as he puts the old-fashioned phone on its cradle, the mood changes. All the children disappear and Maia begins to cry.

I hear her say to Mercy, 'But I don't want to leave – why do we have to leave?'

I hear a door slam and the dream is gone in a flash. I'm still leaning against the bookcase, the orange flower by some miracle still in my palm. But the bookcase is definitely a bookcase – and the carpet isn't a lawn. I feel relieved when I look up to find the ceiling has returned too.

The flower is the same kind that the young woman in the dream, Mercy, placed in the little girl's hair. And the little girl was called Maia . . . that's Nani's name.

Could the flower be Nani's? Perhaps she hid it in here, a long time ago.

I suddenly feel guilty for being in Nani's study, touching her things without permission.

I feel the same tightening of the chest I felt when I first saw the flower – there's something strange about it. It's clearly been hidden away like Nani didn't want anyone to find it.

Fear grips my body as if the emotion of what I've just witnessed has become a part of me. Was it a dream? It seemed to come from nowhere . . . could

I really have somehow made it up?

With trembling fingers I return the flower to its box. The cat has disappeared and I hurry on to my hands and knees and wedge the plinth back in place . . . but keep the box pressed tightly to my chest. I know it's wrong to steal this but I have to try to understand what happened.

Pushing down the guilt, I poke my head into the corridor, scanning for Mum or Nani, but it's deserted. I hurry to my room and hide the box under the bed.

I'm suddenly so tired. I throw myself on the duvet.

Thoughts whirl through my brain and I collapse into a troubled sleep filled with squawking rainbow-coloured birds, children blowing out birthday candles and a cat like a giant tiger prowling through a dense green jungle.

But the sounds I can't get out of my mind are the piercing ring of the phone and Maia's inconsolable cries.

When I wake next morning, I hurriedly scramble to the floor, slide the box with the pressed flower in it from under the bed and flip open the lid. It's still there! I breathe a sigh of relief. Even though I can't explain what happened yesterday, it made me feel closer to Nani. It was as if I was seeing into Nani's past, like her past was slipping into my present.

I'm pretty sure the dream showed me a snapshot from Nani's childhood. I touch the flower again, gently, but this time nothing happens.

I jump on the bed and open the curtains, give myself a big shake. And then I have a brilliant idea! It's to do with Nani and I can't wait to hear what Romeo thinks of it.

I dress and have breakfast in super-quick time. 'Nani,' I call. 'Have you got any spare cushions

I can have?'

'Don't bother your nani while she's trying to get ready,' grumbles Mum.

'What was that, dear?' Nani comes in; her blouse is inside out.

Mum said to act normal so I carry on. 'Do you have any old cushions I can have?'

'I've got a few on my bed – just help yourself.'

I swoop into her room and take the cushions before Mum can complain. 'See you later.'

I call for Romeo and his mum answers the door. She takes a pause from her phone conversation. 'He's not in, love, sorry.'

I feel my forehead crinkle. 'Oh!' I blurt. Maybe he went down to the basement already.

Rushing down the stairs is a bit of a feat with four big cushions, but I manage to waddle-run my way down. I feel for the key we left under the doorway but it's not there. He *is* here already! I bang through the door and drop the cushions.

'Hey, Xanthe!' Romeo has got the other door open and is dragging a pallet into the den.

'Thought you might be here. I called for—' I don't get the chance to finish my sentence because I'm distracted by a girl dragging in a second pallet – and I know exactly who this is.

'You must be Xanthe,' says the girl, extending her hand.

I take a minute to properly look at her. She's not very tall, wears dark-rimmed glasses and her black hair is parted and French braided into two glossy plaits that reach her waist.

'And *you* must be Pria.' My voice wobbles even though I'm trying to control it. I put my hands in my pockets and they make tight fists. My cheeks flare and I give Romeo a fierce look. I wanted to talk to him about the flower and Nani, but it looks like that will have to wait.

Pria awkwardly drops her hand to her side.

'Pria's got some great ideas about the den,' says Romeo, staring at the ground.

'Can I have a word,' I hiss. 'In private!'

I march out of the basement, leaving Pria twiddling with the pallet, and meet Romeo outside the main door.

'I can't believe you,' I begin. 'This was meant to be *our* secret, *our* den. You didn't tell me you'd already been planning things with Prissy Pria.' The last bit slipped out accidentally but I'm so angry I don't care. I feel my face heat up.

'Calm down, Xanthe.'

I try to stomp on his foot but he moves it just in

time. 'Don't tell me to calm down. I didn't realize that you'd be so quick to share this thing that I've only just discovered myself with half the world!'

'I'm sorry!'

I fold my arms tightly.

'It's just that Pria texted me last night about hanging out today.' He looks at me from under his long lashes. 'It just came out – I was excited. I even dreamt about all the things we can do with it.'

I let my arms flop down. 'Just remember who found it.'

My face is still hot. I didn't want to meet Romeo's new friend like this. Straightening my sweatshirt, I shove the door open, Romeo trailing after like a naughty puppy.

When we go back, Pria's resting on the pallet and she springs up immediately. 'Oops,' she says.

I hold out my hand in a businesslike way, hoping I can hide my feelings of hurt and embarrassment. 'Sorry about that, Pria. Let me introduce myself properly. I'm Xanthe, Romeo's best friend from way back.'

'I know,' she replies casually. 'He's told me all about you, and all the adventures you've had since you were little.' She looks around at the basement. 'And this place. It's so cool. It'll look great when we're done.'

Heat sears my cheeks again. This girl Pria is taking over everything. It was 'we', meaning me and Romeo, not 'we' including Pria! But what can I say? 'I brought cushions,' I continue, swallowing down the disappointment. 'We can use the pallets to make a base.'

'Yeah, that's what we thought,' chips in Romeo. He's been standing by the door watching us, kicking at the floor.

'I'm sure my mum can spare some bits and bobs,' says Pria. 'I'll bring them next time. And in the meantime I brought stuff so we can paint some murals on the walls.'

'Pria's a great artist,' says Romeo.

She blushes and flicks her plaits back. 'I'll paint some Ghibli characters if you like, to cheer the place up.'

I dart Romeo a look. 'Sounds good. And maybe we can have some historical stuff too. I don't know if Romeo told you,' I say, 'but I love history!'

Pria pulls a face.

My anger flares again and this time I don't stop myself. 'I think you could show a little respect. Fair enough that you don't like history but *I* do, and after all *I* was the one who found this den.' I take a deep breath of cold air. 'My nani was an archaeologist and she taught me how important history is – after all, how can we understand anything about ourselves if we don't know where we came from?'

Romeo clears his throat. 'It's good to have passions.' He dives into his rucksack. 'And we're all different – I brought biscuits!' He fishes out a giant-size packet of chocolate digestives and hands them out.

There's an uncomfortable silence as we all take a biscuit.

'So,' begins Pria. 'What sort of mural design shall we do?'

'Are you sure you can do the Ghibli figures?' I ask, still feeling annoyed. 'They're a bit hard to draw.'

'I can do it.' Pria is very sure of herself.

'Anyway, like I said, I want to have something from the past. If you *don't* mind.' I crunch the biscuit. 'Can you imagine what might have been here before they built these tower blocks? There might have been all sorts of things.'

'Like Vikings and stuff?' says Romeo.

'Yeah – but the Anglo-Saxons before that and tools from the Bronze Age have been found in Nottingham as well. There's loads of history here. There might even be some ancient burial sites, right under our feet.'

'There's plenty of wall space,' says Romeo. 'We can do both. It's just about making it brighter, isn't it?'

I'm determined it won't be all about what Pria wants. 'Maybe we can have Studio Ghibli for Pria, some historical scenes and artefacts for me . . . and things you like, Romeo . . . a peregrine falcon maybe?'

'I'll start here.' Pria takes her pencil and begins on one of the walls. 'I've got some photos from *My Neighbor Totoro* on my phone.'

'And I'll bring some images of what I want too.'

Pria doesn't waste time and begins drawing the scene right away. She picks the one with the cute forest spirit Totoro sitting on a branch above a river with Satsuki and her sister Mei.

'That's a great choice,' says Romeo, peering at Pria's phone. 'I love the countryside in the background.'

'We could start filling in the river if you like,' I say.

Pria's really organized – I can't believe she's even brought paints – and pulls out some old shirts from her bag to protect us from splats.

Romeo puts on some music and at last the atmosphere chills as I begin to relax and get busy with the mural.

Even though the mural is hardly started you can see the difference it makes to the den already. Romeo was right, Pria's an amazing artist, all the Ghibli characters look incredible. But I can't help feeling irritated by her – she's so annoyingly perfect!

The morning passes quickly and we pause for a rest. Pria checks a message on her phone. 'It's Mum. I'd better get going.'

'We've made a really good start,' I say.

'Let's come back tomorrow,' says Romeo, squashing the half-packet of biscuits back in his bag and taking off his painty shirt.

Pria grabs her helmet and heads up to collect her bike from the courtyard. 'I'll leave the paint stuff here,' she calls down. 'Nice to meet you, Xanthe.'

Later, I take plates and cutlery up to the roof garden and put them on the table, ready for supper.

'There are some plug plants here,' says Mum, handing me a trowel. She's been weeding the garden, and it already looks much tidier.

I take the French beans and dig them a nice hole, gathering them in groups of four to trail up the poles once they get going.

'Wow, it's going to look great in no time,' says Mum, peering at the seed packets.

I take the end of the hose and begin sprinkling water over the newly planted borders. It's all looking much neater and I know there's more to do, but it makes me happy that we're slowly making things better.

We're helping Nani with something that means so much to her. The scents of flowers and damp earth are returning. I watch a bumblebee hover over the wild red poppies before zooming through the tall banana plants and disappearing further into the garden.

Nani arrives carrying glasses on a tray and sets them down on the table before dishing out the food. 'Come on, you two, it's all ready.'

I sit by Nani.

I remember what Mum said yesterday about helping Nani remember her past and maybe making a life story with her. Perhaps I should be more direct this time about finding out about Uganda? Nani's relaxed and happy right now, after all. She might be receptive. So I launch right in.

'What happened in Uganda, Nani? Why did you have to leave?'

She grips her fork tightly and her mouth makes an odd straight line like her lips are stuck together. 'Don't ask me about that, Xanthe! I just don't want to talk about it.'

Mum's face has gone all weird too, like she knows I've stepped in a place I shouldn't have.

'Sorry, Nani.' My heart begins to hammer. 'I didn't mean to upset you. I – I thought you might like to remember.'

'No!' she says loudly. 'I never want to remember that.'

The mood's ruined and I stay quiet through supper, thinking about what happened earlier with Romeo and Pria. It seems I'm upsetting everyone today. My throat feels tight and I push my food around on the plate.

Making an excuse, I leave the table and go to my room. I lie on the bed watching the sunset spread purple light against the walls. I haven't brushed my teeth but I don't care. Putting on my pyjamas I pull the duvet tight. I didn't even get the chance to tell Romeo my idea.

The doorknob rattles and Mum comes in.

'What's the matter, pumpkin?' she says, sitting on the bed.

Tears drip down my cheeks. 'Everything,' I sniff. 'Romeo's got a new friend and I'm worried that he'll like her better than me, and whenever I try to ask Nani about Uganda I manage to upset her rather than making her feel better. Even though, when she does talk about it, she seems so much more herself.'

Mum wipes my tears and snuggles in next to me. 'You and Romeo will always have a special thing,' she begins. 'But it's normal to meet new people. You'll both change – especially when you start secondary in September. But the important thing is your friendship is strong. And as for Nani, I think some of those memories are still so difficult.'

'Why *did* Nani have to move so quickly from Uganda?'

Mum sighs. 'It's complicated and I don't know all the details. My dad told me a little but not much. It was such a difficult time. The government changed in Uganda and the leader decided that all the Asian community should leave.'

'But Mum, Nani was *born* in Uganda – she was Ugandan too. So how could he do that?'

Mum clears her throat and looks around the room. 'The leader at that time, Idi Amin, was angry about the differences between the African Ugandans and the Asian Ugandans and how the Indian people had been introduced into their country by the British Empire. He felt they were doing better than native Ugandans and that this wasn't fair.'

My head's spinning with the historical details. I

know there's a lot to understand, but I can't help focusing on the human story right in front of me. 'But Nani didn't get to go to Makerere University – *that* was unfair! And she had to leave her home.'

'And Grandpapa – Nani's papa, your *great*-grandfather – had to leave his job in the civil service.'

I pause for a moment, feeling a mixture of sadness and anger swirling around inside me. 'It all sounds really hard and I can understand now why Nani gets upset by it.'

'Only fifty pounds, Grandpapa used to say,' continues Mum. 'I can hear him now: "I built our life on fifty pounds!"'

'So they could only bring fifty pounds for the whole family?' The shock hits me. 'But that's nothing.'

'I know.' She kisses me on the forehead. 'But maybe you can help Nani remember the good times. Perhaps just steer clear of Uganda?'

'OK. Night, Mum.'

She switches the light off and clicks the door closed. 'Night, baby.'

Finding out that Nani's family had to create a whole new life with as little as £50 is unbelievable. It's the amount I collected altogether for my last birthday and it makes me realize how tough it would have been and how little I really know about Nani's old life.

I know Mum said to keep off the Ugandan topic but I keep remembering the flower and what happened when I held it. This makes me think something powerful and strange is going on – like it's time for those memories to come out, even though they might be painful.

When Nani talked about finding the rubies and feathers she lit up and her thoughts were so vivid and clear. It's as if those childhood memories leaked into the flower and bloomed out when I held it for the first time.

It's not quite dark outside and a sliver of brightness peeks from under the curtain. I imagine twelve-year-old Nani in Uganda, gathering her things but having to leave her precious feather, the special lucky one as red as winter sun, and I can't stop another tear from sneaking down my nose.

I take the flower from its box under my bed and hold it gently in my palm like I did before, but however much I close my eyes and imagine myself back in the daydream under the flame tree, nothing happens.

8

Early next morning, I hear a mewling sound. Blinking open my eyes I rub at the sleep crystals edging my lashes. The cat is here again, standing in the wedge of the doorway, lacy sunlight lighting up its swirled and patterned fur. 'Hello, you.' I study it carefully.

It looks like a tiger with its dark brown and yellow stripes. I know cats go wherever someone feeds them so I expect Nani's been doing that, but I still can't figure out how it's getting in. A long pink tongue suddenly pops from its mouth, revealing sharp white teeth. Yawning, it tosses its head towards me and fixes me with those eyes as bright as shining sapphires.

I leap to the floor and reach for the silver name tag that I didn't notice before, but it turns its head so I can't quite see. I crouch closer and read the tag quickly before it moves away again.

'You're called Leo? Well, at least I know your name now.'

He patters out of the bedroom and, as if he has a strange power over me, I follow him into the hallway and out on to the landing. His shadow-shape darkens the floor and spreads before us towards the stairwell.

It's still early and everything is gloomy quiet; the corridor lights buzz like annoyed insects. I follow Leo all the way down fifteen flights of stairs until we're outside the basement den.

The den looks eerie in the weak morning light, the sketchy Ghibli figures staring spookily from the walls. The boiler gives a loud gurgle that makes me jump and the cat begins sniffing around the packed earth to one side of it, bending his head low to the ground and practically hissing.

'What's the matter? Have you brought me all the way down here to help you hunt for rats?' I rub my arms. Even though it's warm in the den a sudden shiver prickles my spine.

Leo starts making a weird purring noise and paws at the dirt, digging his claws in and scratching the ground. I kneel beside him and watch. I've never heard of cats digging like this before, as if searching for something, but that's definitely what he's doing.

I wonder again what might have been here before the flats, before the city was built. A flutter begins to swim around my belly. There might be prehistoric axes made from precious stone buried under here, metal swords used to fight off enemies or pretty Anglo-Saxon jewellery just waiting to be found!

I spy an old screwdriver beside the boiler and join the cat. Perhaps Leo is leading me to some ancient artefact and I begin to get excited. Imagine the headline: *Schoolgirl Discovers Ancient Burial Site.*

We both dig at the surface of the soil for ages, but we don't make much progress; the ground is pretty solid.

'I'll have to come back later with proper tools,' I tell Leo.

I think about how much I want to tell Romeo . . . but then I remember the face Pria pulled when I talked about history and feel a niggle of annoyance. Romeo will tell her if I tell him. Maybe I don't want to share this with them. Maybe I don't want them both commenting, telling me they don't believe there's anything down there. I drag the pallet sofa across the spot.

I'll dig here in secret and when I find treasure, they'll be so impressed and will wish they could share in the glory.

The cat scoots away through the doorway, and in a blink he's swallowed up by the gloom.

Back in the flat, the curtains are still drawn and neither Mum or Nani are awake yet. I go into the kitchen and make myself a hot chocolate.

And then I start thinking about Nani and how we both love history, and what if there actually *is* something important in the basement? Imagine how proud Nani would be if I discovered something historical right under her very own tower block.

Instead of going back to bed with the hot chocolate, I creep up to the roof garden, find a metal trowel and head back to the basement.

I've still got time before everyone starts their daily routines and I push back the pallet sofa ceremoniously. I think of all the history programmes I've seen and all the news reports of people finding the most incredible treasures in their back gardens, uncovering amazing unexpected stories of past lives. Like finding the remains of Richard III under a car park – an actual king buried under a car park! That was only down the road in Leicester – I start to get a tingly feeling that I might find something special here.

Forcing the trowel into the hard earth, I begin to dig. It's still hard, but slowly I manage to edge the trowel in further, shifting fine layers of compacted earth.

I'll have to find myself a brush so I can be like a real archaeologist – you have to be gentle with ancient artefacts. I take a moment to touch the ground like I'm hoping to connect with whatever might be down there. I don't know if it's my imagination but I sense a faint tremor, like my fingertips are connecting with an ancient energy deep below the flats, and I say a little prayer.

9

I keep scraping the earth back, scoop it into a box with the trowel and empty it into the flower beds in the small courtyard outside the den. I've made good progress and even though the soil is still hard and stuck together the ground isn't flat any more.

The clank of the lift shaft startles me – it must be later than I thought. Hurrying to tidy up, I scramble the loose soil back into the hole, drop in the trowel and cover it with the pallet.

I slip out of the den and head back up the stairwell, taking the steps two at a time until I'm right at the fifteenth floor. Taking a few seconds to bring my breath back to normal, I lean against the door to Nani's flat, listening to waking voices in Romeo's house.

As quietly as I can, I click open Nani's door and step inside. Mum's in the kitchen, so I dart into the bathroom to wash the dirt off my hands. I catch a glimpse of my face in the mirror and allow myself a satisfied smile as I imagine the headlines again.

'Xanthe, is that you? What are you up to?'

I twist the tap off and join Mum in the kitchen. 'Nothing – morning,' I say, rubbing at my eyes and yawning.

She studies me carefully. 'You could have had a lie-in.' She sips her tea. 'It's still early. Remember what I said about not upsetting Nani in any way. Don't do anything out of the ordinary.'

'Of course I won't. I'm just busying myself with one of my projects.'

'Mmm . . .' sighs Mum.

My brain is whirring with possibilities, imagining the find and wondering what it might be and how the papers will be all over it. I push it to the back of my mind for the moment. Slotting a couple of slices of bread into the toaster, I heat the hot chocolate from earlier.

'What are you going to do today?'

'I thought I might make a start on Nani's life story.' I fix Mum's gaze. 'Except the early bit, of course. I want to do everything I can to help her.'

'We all do,' she says, staring into her tea.

I'm about to ask Mum about Treetops Lodge. It

makes me so cross to even think Mum would consider it, but the worry frown appears between Mum's eyebrows again and I know a row would upset Nani – it's better to help her my way, then I can show Mum she's just fine here. I cross my arms and feel stronger.

'Dad sends his love. I spoke to him this morning. He's got a big building project on – but I said you'd call him this evening.'

I spread peanut butter on the toast and slice banana on top. 'Yeah – I'll call him later.'

There's a rap on the front door and when I jump up to answer, Romeo's face is on the other side.

'I'm not around today,' he says. 'But we can get on with finishing the murals tomorrow if you like.'

My stomach twists. 'OK,' I reply and wonder if he's meeting up with Pria. If so, I bet they'll talk about me.

His mum appears from their flat, Evan and Mila chasing each other again. 'We're taking a picnic to the city farm,' explains Mrs Wilson, 'to see if we can tire these two out with some fresh air.' I feel a rush of relief.

'Later,' says Romeo.

'Have fun!'

Back in the flat, I finish off breakfast and take

Nani a cup of tea to her room. With Romeo out all day, I could easily spend more time on the dig – it's such a great chance. But the thrill of the thought flies off like a feather in the wind as a pang of guilt leaps at me. *What am I thinking? I should be putting Nani first, not myself.*

I place the tea by Nani's bed. 'Shall we start making your life story today, Nani?' I say gently.

'I'd love that.' Nani sits up in bed and folds her hands around the mug of tea.

We set up in the kitchen and spread the paper, pens and pencils out on the table. 'Which part would you like to talk about today?' I ask Nani.

I remember how upset she got before so I'll keep away from Uganda, even though it's the only thing I want to talk about. I still don't understand what happened in Nani's study with the pressed flower – perhaps it was just my imagination. After all, when I held it again nothing happened.

'Are you OK, Xanthe?' asks Nani. 'You're looking very thoughtful.'

'Sorry, Nani, my mind just wandered off for a minute. Shall we start with growing up in Nottingham?'

'That sounds good,' she says.

'So just tell me anything, Nani, and I'll scribble it down. It doesn't have to be in any order – just the things that made you happy.'

I listen carefully to Nani and record it as quickly as I can. She tells me about her secondary school. It was a girls' school and they had a smart uniform with red-and-white striped shirts, grey pleated skirts and a grey blazer with red braiding on it.

'I won the history prize,' she says, sounding really proud. 'And my best friend was a lovely girl called Michelle.' She begins to laugh. 'We got up to all sorts but we were inseparable – a bit like you and Romeo.'

For the rest of the day I work on *Nani's Life Story Part One*. We take breaks for drinks and something to eat and all the while I can tell it's making Nani feel better. She's looking less stressed and there's a new sparkle in her eyes.

Nani's memories are healing her but I can't help feeling there's something missing – Uganda. I feel a tug of conflict. I know I promised Mum I'd steer right away from talking about it, but what if facing those sad memories is just the thing Nani needs?

I push the thoughts away. I should be happy that Nani seems relaxed. When she gets tired, I collect everything together in a shoebox for later.

All day my mind has been distracted and I've hardly thought about the basement dig. But now it all pings back. I leave Nani to have a snooze and slip into the bathroom where I root around in the under-sink cupboard, searching for something to clean up the artefacts I'm convinced I'm going to find. Among the half-filled bottles of shampoo and blocks of lavender soap I find a small soft brush and some rags. I put everything into an empty cotton bag.

'I'm just going for a walk, Mum,' I yell, as I bang the front door closed.

I hurry down the stairs to the den and put my tools to one side. Late afternoon sun spreads through the window, glinting on the murals and floor.

Dragging the pallet away from the hole I pick up the trowel, my hand quivering, and begin to dig again. I'm concentrating really hard, imagining once more what I might find if I keep digging. I stab the trowel into the soil over and over, emptying it on to the floor beside me. I've only been at it a short while, when I hear a shuffling by the den door and the sound of someone swinging it open.

10

It's Romeo! Romeo and I both jump out of our skins. Heart pounding, I jump from the floor and begin jiggling about in front of the hole I've been digging, desperately trying to hide it. 'What are you doing, sneaking up on people like that!'

'You nearly gave me a heart attack,' replies Romeo, clearly shocked to see anyone down here. 'And what are *you* doing?'

He takes a few steps towards me and I don't know how I'm going to hide the hole. I try to hook the pallet from behind and pull it to cover what I've been up to, but Romeo skirts round my back.

'What are you doing?' he says, staring into the dark hole.

There's nothing I can do but flop down on the pallet instead. 'Romeo – I think there might be something down there.'

'What do you mean . . . ? Like rats or old pipes?' He's looking at me in total disbelief.

I flush with annoyance. 'Like some sort of ancient treasure, that's what I mean.'

Romeo sniffs and sits beside me on the pallet. 'And why are you hiding it? I thought we were a gang.'

I ignore the question. Me and Romeo *were* a gang. He doesn't understand how Pria has changed things. 'It was really weird,' I begin. 'Remember the cat I told you about, the one that's been hanging about Nani's flat?' Romeo's nodding. 'Well, he's been . . . showing me things.'

Romeo raises an eyebrow. 'Showing you things?'

I can tell it sounds really weird. 'Just listen. The thing is there's something strange about this cat. He appears and disappears in the oddest way. The other day he got into the flat and led me to Nani's study. Right to a pressed flower hidden behind the bottom of the bookshelf. The box was covered in dust as if it hadn't been touched for years.'

'What's so unusual about that?'

'That's not all. When I held the flower in my palm I had a sort of flash of a memory, but I'm sure it was Nani's memory from when she was in Uganda.'

'Whoa, whoa, slow down.'

I take a moment to catch my breath, a tremble fills my body. 'The thing is, I think I saw the moment when Nani found out she had to leave Uganda. I could feel her sadness.'

Romeo blinks. 'This is a lot to take in . . . so you're saying that this flower is holding your nani's forgotten memories?'

'Not forgotten but pushed down because it was too painful to remember.' I'm pleased that Romeo isn't totally dismissing this because it does sound a bit way out. 'I wanted to tell you as soon as it happened but I couldn't because you were down here with Pria.' The hurt stabs again.

'Well . . . thanks for sharing with me now. Look, I'm your friend Xan and you can tell me anything.'

'Yeah – thanks. I've got this theory that if only I can get Nani to talk about what happened in Uganda it will help her.'

Romeo nods thoughtfully. 'As my dad says – better out than in!' He pauses. 'But how does any of this relate to the hole you're digging? Did the cat show you that too?'

I sigh. 'He's called Leo. I found a tag around his neck and yes, earlier today I followed him down here and he began pawing the ground. I started thinking that maybe he was sensing something and that there actually is an important object down there.'

'You never know,' he says, an amused note in his voice. 'They found Richard III's bones under a car park not far from here.'

'Don't tease me.'

'I'm not teasing – I know how much history means to you.' He glances down at the hole. 'How about I help you with it?'

I feel my hard edges crumble. 'The thing is, I don't want anyone else to know. I don't want Pria jinxing this even before I've started.'

His expression hardens. 'Give Pria a break, Xan. I know she shouldn't have pulled that face when you mentioned how much you love history but she's a good person, she wouldn't jinx this – plus, she's having a tough time at the moment.'

I'm annoyed at how quick he is to defend her. I'm going through a tough time too! But I don't want to argue with Romeo so I back down and deflect. 'Well, I'd love your help. It might be nothing – but just think of all the possibilities. There could be *anything* down there and when we find it, can you imagine the excitement? Nani was the one who sparked my love for history and she'd just go wild if there really were something wonderful hidden below her home.'

'OK,' says Romeo. 'It can be our secret.'

'Thanks, Rome – shall we keep going then?' I hand Romeo the trowel. 'I brought a brush and rags and everything, in case we dig anything up. I'll use the screwdriver for the minute and you can have the trowel, but I'll bring the garden fork next time we come down.'

'The hole's quite deep already,' says Romeo. 'We might even need a shovel.'

He's right. The earth I dug out this morning is already making a half-moon dip in the hole beneath our feet. As we scrape and pull more soil away it looks even more mysterious and full of possibilities.

When I stand back to assess our progress the hole is about the size of a big box. 'How was the city farm?' I ask, feeling pleased.

'A bit boring for me but the littlies had fun. And more importantly they might be quiet later and give Mum a break. Honestly, Xan, they're full on.'

We chat away while we work on the dig, both of us on hands and knees leaning over the hole, Romeo with the trowel and me with the screwdriver. We take the loose soil out to the courtyard and the next time I glance at my watch it's nearly six thirty.

'I'd better get back,' I say. 'You too? Mum'll wonder where I've got to. I told her I was going for a walk.'

'Yeah – I only popped down to bring a couple of old throws that Mum said we could have, to make it more comfy.'

'We'd better tidy up a bit.'

'True – it looks a bit of a wreck in here.' Romeo grabs a broom and begins sweeping.

I take a final boxful of soil outside but when I come back, it's like I don't want to stop digging. I pick up the trowel and push it into the hole that's looking full of possibility.

Romeo has his hand on the door handle. 'Come on, Xan, we can come back tomorrow once Pria has gone.'

'Just a few more minutes.'

'And we've just tidied up.'

'Sorry – I'll sort it.' I scoop trowels of soil and dump it on the edge while Romeo sits on the cushions and watches.

I suddenly feel something chip against the trowel and when I force the tip further into the darkness, I feel it again.

'I think I've found something,' I squeal.

'What? Really?'

I keep going and in the dusky light of the den, in the dark dirt of the hole, I see something.

Romeo peers over my shoulder. 'What is it?'

'It looks like shells . . . rows of them.' I feel my heart speed up. The shells are embedded in the soil; they're each the size of my small finger with ridged lines fanning out along each one.

'C-can you get the rags so I can lay them out please?' I take the brush, like I've seen archaeologists do on TV, and clear the area around each one before levering one of the pale shells out.

I allow myself a skip of satisfaction and feel a sort of tingle in my fingers as I hold the shell in my palm and bring it close to my ear. An eerie lap of a vast sea fills my head with its mysterious sound and sweeps me away . . . away to a far-off place.

I feel myself sway as the firm floor of the den seems strangely softer. When I look down it's like the concrete has disappeared and in its place is golden sand. I'm suddenly not wearing trainers because when I wiggle my toes grains of sand slide between them. The grey concrete walls disappear and deep-green palm trees burst into view. I look up and shield my eyes against a blazing sun that appears above me instead of the basement ceiling. The entire space is filled with warmth and bright light and fresh salty air. I'm not in the basement any more but on the most beautiful summery beach.

The water shushes gently against the shoreline. The

sea is an incredible deep emerald green and small waves rush towards the shore. There's a hand-painted sign that reads 'Lake Victoria Pleasure Rides' and it's stuck into the sand with an arrow pointing to a large boat with rows of seats.

Halfway down the beach a family with a big picnic spread on a blue tablecloth are joking and having fun. A little way away two girls are running at the waves and jumping over them. They both wear striped swimming costumes and look about the same age, around twelve.

There's a cat that looks like Leo by their feet, but they don't seem to notice it as it jumps away from the shore, leaving deep imprints in the sand.

One of the girls has a bucket in her hand and she sits on the beach. She pushes her fingers deep into the sand and each time she brings out a few shells and puts them in the bucket. Now the other girl walks a little further away and finds more shells and she brings them to her friend, who collects them all together.

They play this game for a while and each time there's a new shell, the girl sitting on the sand examines it carefully before putting it with the others.

Eventually, they tip all the shells on to the beach and make patterns with them. A woman wearing a colourful scarf wrapped around her hair calls out:

'Maia, Manjula, come and get food! There's chicken muchomos – your favourite, Maia.'

The two girls gather all the white shells into the bucket and run giggling towards the young woman. She takes one of the shells in her palm and holds it out, the ridges fanning out like fingers.

The girls kneel on the tablecloth and help themselves to food.

The girl called Manjula suddenly looks sad, setting down her food before she's even taken a bite. 'I won't be able to play with you any more,' she says. Although she's speaking in another language, I can understand.

'Why not?' Maia's voice trembles.

'My papa says it's not safe here. We're moving to Canada.'

The girls hug each other, their cheeks wet. Behind them the tall palm trees rustle in the breeze. On the water, brightly coloured fishing boats bob along the waves and seabirds dip their yellow beaks into the lake before a loud clap makes them take to the blue skies. I watch as the birds flutter off, getting smaller and smaller.

11

When I open my eyes I realize that I'm still in the basement.

'Xanthe?' Romeo's voice interrupts my thoughts. 'Are you OK? You went all weird for a minute.'

I lean against him. 'That was really strange. It happened again – like it did with the flower. It was like I was dreaming. I saw the day the shells were collected – it was the same day Maia's friend Manjula said they were leaving Uganda. Maia – Nani – was devastated.'

'You said you came down here really early,' says Romeo. 'I think you're pretty tired.'

Romeo is speaking in a way that tells me that although he's trying to be understanding, he's not actually sure about any of this.

I jump in quickly. 'I don't understand any of this

either, it seems so incredible, but what if both of these objects – the flower and the shell – were Nani's? Somehow, I'm being shown something important. I know it.'

I blink at the treasure in front of us and notice how each shell has been laid in a careful pattern.

'You think your nani buried these?' Romeo bends down to get a closer look. 'It definitely doesn't seem like they were just thrown in. They're arranged too precisely.'

I grab my phone and take a photo. 'I'm going to record everything about this dig, just like a proper archaeologist.' I feel the wide grin on my face and a tickle of excitement under my ribs. Something deep in my bones tells me this is a really important find.

We carry on digging and after an hour or so me and Romeo have unearthed twenty shells from the hole under the basement den. I take more photos before carefully brushing each shell off and laying them all out on the cloth.

We're so absorbed that we don't hear any footsteps approaching. Instead, the door to the den suddenly bangs and we startle.

It's Pria.

'Hey, guys. I know it's late but I wanted to drop something off for . . .' She trails off, swings her bike helmet to and fro and stares at the hole. 'What's that?'

I send a jittery glance over to Romeo. I don't know what to say. I didn't want Pria to be here and I feel my cheeks turn red.

'We've been digging,' says Romeo, like it's the most normal thing ever to dig down into a basement.

'Umm . . . yeah?' Pria looks totally confused.

There's nothing for it. We have to tell her. I breathe out. 'Look . . . we've found something amazing.' I jut my chin out and cross my arms over my chest in case I need to defend myself.

Pria walks over to the shells that are arranged carefully on the rags. She covers her mouth and lets out a giggle. 'These? They just look like junk to me. I mean it's not exactly treasure, is it? Or even anything old.'

I feel my temper rise. 'When you're interested in history, Pria, you have to find out the story behind each object. These shells were laid in a special pattern and could tell us a lot about the past.'

She bends down and picks one of the shells up. 'This looks like any old shell – what does it tell us about the past? That some kid went to the beach and buried the shells down here for some random reason. It doesn't sound very *historical* to me!'

'Don't touch that!' I yell, prising it from her fingers.

'Keep your hair on. It's only a boring old shell.'

I spin to face her. 'First you muscled your way between me and Romeo, and now you're taking over the den, coming and going whenever you want. But actually, I found this place and if anyone should be in charge of it it's me. And – and I don't know if I want any of your silly Ghibli paintings in here.'

Romeo steps between us. 'Come on, you two.'

'No, Romeo. Pria has no right, and anyway I've got a much better idea for the basement.' This isn't how I imagined it would be when I told Romeo my idea, but I clear my throat and launch in. 'I'd like to set it up as a museum.'

They both look at me as if I've said something beyond strange.

'Well, that sounds as boring as those shells.' Pria shares a smirk with Romeo.

'A museum?' he says. 'Really, Xanthe? This is meant to be our chill-out space and I have to agree with Pria, it does sound a bit . . . well . . . boring.'

I can't believe Romeo is taking her side – after everything. 'You don't know anything.' Hot tears flash down my cheeks but I brush them away. 'I've shared it all with you, the special things that mean so much to me, things I know aren't easy to believe, but I trusted you. Now you've got someone to laugh at me with – like I'm just a big joke.'

'Xan!' Romeo tries to edge closer but I shove him away.

'And as for you, Pria, you've tried your best to put me and my ideas down – have you never heard that three is a crowd? Well, you're welcome to each other.'

Neither of them say a thing, just stand there gawping at me.

Salt-sting blurs my eyes and my anger is out of control now. I bundle up the shells, barge past them both, hurl myself out of the door, rush up the stairs and let my anger roar free, but with each step it turns to disappointment.

How could Romeo side with Pria? I thought he'd understand why I wanted to create a museum and why it would be the best idea for the basement because it meant so much to me and to Nani.

By the time I've reached the top I feel weak with all the shouting and pause on the landing. I flick a look down the winding stairwell, but Romeo clearly doesn't care enough to see how I'm feeling and sadness scratches a tight place in my chest.

12

slip into the flat quietly and take the shells to my room.

Pulling the pressed-flower box from under my bed, I lift the lid and place the shells carefully inside, laying all twenty of them one beside the other around the flower.

Having the fight with Romeo makes me feel closer to Nani, and while he's busy making new best friends with Pria, at least it gives me time to focus on these objects I've found.

I don't need him anyway.

I crouch against the carpet and study them closely – it was pretty weird to find shells under the basement. The way they were laid out was like the finishing touch to something.

My brain begins to whirr with all the possibilities and I think about how archaeologists are like detectives, who discover so much even from the way artefacts are found.

I run my finger along the fine grooves of the shells that still have traces of soil clinging to them. Peering closely, I notice their pale whiteness tinged with a pretty blue, and imagine again what they are and why they were hidden below the tower block.

They are like the sort of shells you find on a beach, small but perfect, home to a cockle maybe or a bigger sea creature.

The first vision with the flower was so vivid, and it was the same with the shell when I held it in my palm down in the basement. I take one of the shells again and try to bring the memory back, but it's no good. I can remember the vision and what happened, but I can't bring back that sense of being right there on the beach with Maia's best friend Manjula, or the thump of fear Maia felt when she heard the terrible news.

I wonder again if these objects belonged to Nani – in fact, I feel certain they did. She brought them from Uganda. Then, she hid the flower and buried these shells – perhaps because they conjured painful memories. She hid the objects away just like she buried the memories deep inside her.

But now the memories are seeping out.

I feel a flutter in my belly.

I have to treat these objects properly, carefully.

I take a piece of A4 paper and across the top I write 'TOWER BLOCK FIND, XANTHE SHARP'. And then I write the date really clearly underneath. Taking tiny bits of Blu-Tack, I stick the paper to the lid of the box.

I remember the vision, the tingle I felt when I touched the first shell. What if there's more waiting to be discovered – maybe even beneath where the shells were buried? Excitement buzzes at my belly again and I can't wait to go back and dig deeper. Perhaps whatever I find will transport me to another place like the flower and the shells.

There's a tap on my door and I push the box under the bed. It's Nani.

'Your mum was frantic,' she says, wringing her hands together. 'She didn't know where you were. You'd better nip in there and calm her down.'

Suddenly the fight with Romeo rushes at my insides and tears spring to my eyes.

'Hey – what's this?' Nani takes her cotton hankie and wipes my cheek.

'I had a fight with Romeo,' I blurt between sobs.

'Oh, darling.' Nani puts an arm around me and draws me to her. 'That's it, don't hold it in.'

When my sobs have quietened down I tell her how I feel, even though I can't tell her why we fought. 'The thing is, we never usually fight, it's just that he's got himself a new friend while I've been away and it's really hard not having him to myself.'

'I had a best friend too when I was your age. She was called Manjula,' Nani says.

I feel a thrill of recognition. That's the girl from the memory!

'Did you ever fight?'

'We were thick as thieves – we'd known each other since we were babies, just like you two.' Nani's face shadows for a moment, but then in the next beat it's back to normal. 'You and Romeo are so close but you have to accept that other people will want to be your friends too. Maybe you should be the brave one, the first to say sorry.'

I'm about to say how it was all Pria's fault but I think Nani's right. 'It just made me so sad, Nani, but I'll try to make it right.'

'Good girl – friendships are the most precious thing; you have to guard them. Come on, let's see what your mum's up to.'

Talking to Nani has made me feel so much better. Being able to share what happened really helped.

My face must be puffy and red because Mum

stares at me with her kind eyes.

'Me and Romeo had a bit of an argument, but I talked it through with Nani and I'm going to sort it.'

'So that's where you were.' She puts a hand on my shoulder. 'His mum came round here, as she wondered where on earth he'd got to. We were about to come hunting for you both.'

'Sorry, Mum, promise I'll let you know next time.' I feel bad making Mum worry about me as well as Nani.

'Anyway,' she says cheerfully, 'you must be starving. I've got veggie fajitas for dinner.'

Even though the light is fading, we eat on the roof garden and watch the swallows as they swoop over our heads, collecting insects from the plants that wave in the soft breeze. The sky turns to copper and the warmth from the sun makes it one of those almost perfect summer evenings. A pang of sadness tugs at my chest as I wish Romeo was here too so we could make up.

'I hear you started on Nani's life story.'

'Yes, we did – didn't we, Nani?' I say, trying to distract myself.

'Part One,' she says. 'I so enjoyed telling you about it.'

'I really loved it too.'

'By the way Nani, I saw the cat you said keeps coming in.'

'Oh, that cat!' laughs Nani. 'He's such a rascal.'

Mum frowns.

Nani's eyes go twinkly. 'Little Leo – tiger-striped and full of mischief.'

'He really is adorable,' I agree.

'I just want to show Xanthe something.' Mum beckons me over and leads me towards the flame tree, which is looking so much better than when we arrived, its plump leaves spreading star-like shadows on the gravel.

'Xanthe . . . Leo was the cat Nani had when she was little.'

I blink. 'No, Mum, it's—'

But Mum cuts me off. 'I'm not cross. I know you're just trying to keep Nani happy. But we have to keep things really simple for her. Please don't mention the fantasy cat – we don't want to confuse her. OK?'

Mum seems really serious so I nod, even though I know Leo is real – he's not a fantasy cat!

'Good. Let's get back to dinner, then,' she says, smiling.

13

All night long the thought of the dig in the basement burrows into my mind, snake-like, sparking the corners of my imagination. In my dreams I discover all sorts of things: Viking helmets, bronze bracelets with twisted patterns, bags crammed with medieval coins.

I toss and turn, crumpling the bedclothes, and when I wake, the duvet is twisted around me, a tight coil padded with feathers. I'm hot and wriggle myself free, throw the covers to the floor and leap from the bed. Outside, heavy grey clouds cover the patches of pale blue; rain is slanting from the sky, drenching the windows, water beading along the glass.

I shovel down breakfast and scrawl Mum a note in case she worries again. I know what I have to do this morning: apologize to Romeo and Pria – like Nani said, friendships are as precious as treasure and I have to look after mine. I'm about to leave the flat when there's a timid knock on the door.

I click open the lock to find Romeo and Pria waiting outside.

There's an awkward pause.

'Sorry, Xanthe.' Pria lowers her eyes. 'I shouldn't have made fun of you about the museum idea. I feel awful.'

'I should've realized how much it meant to you,' says Romeo, stepping closer. 'I'm sorry.'

'I'm sorry too,' I say to both of them, my eyes darting from one to the other. 'I was just going to come over and say so. I'm sorry I yelled at you both.'

'It's OK. I wanted to come round sooner,' says Romeo, 'but Mum had a thousand chores for me to do.'

'I actually think a museum is a cool idea,' Pria says. 'I've been mean because I really wanted to be part of your group, and it felt like you didn't want me.'

I can tell she's really trying – she looks upset. 'I'm sorry, Pria. I really was leaving you out. Thank you about the museum.' I've got to explain what I've been thinking. 'The thing is, it wouldn't be just any old museum.' I swallow. 'I wanted to create a museum for Nani, for her life story. We've started collecting things from her past anyway. I thought it would be such a great surprise to fill the museum with special objects and photos to help her remember her life.'

Pria looks genuinely moved. 'That's such a kind thing to do.'

I don't really understand how one minute she's so mean and the next she can be so nice. Then I realize it's because I've included her – for once, I haven't been trying to hide stuff.

Her eyes flash as if she's thinking of something. 'Um . . . instead of the Ghibli, why don't I draw murals from your nani's past?'

I study her carefully in case she's just saying it because Romeo's here. 'W-would you really do that?'

'Yeah, sure.'

I look away at the floor.

'She means it, don't you, Pria?' Romeo adds.

She nods. 'Course.'

'Well, that would be amazing – thank you.'

Romeo is looking relieved; he's obviously really glad we've stopped arguing. I feel bad, realizing that all he ever wanted was for his two friends to get along. Why should I have held that against him?

Pria lets out a long sigh. 'I'm glad we're not arguing any more. I've had enough of that at home.'

She must see the confusion on my face because she explains. 'My parents are getting a divorce.' Her eyes well up and she stares away. This must've been what Romeo meant about her going through a hard time.

'I'm sorry,' I say gently.

'It's one of the reasons I like hanging out here. It'll be good to focus on the museum with you both.'

I feel bad for arguing with Pria when all the time she's been so unhappy. I'm determined to be especially kind to her from now on, maybe invite her to see the garden.

But for now . . . we all need to shake things up. 'Anyone up for the Staircase Race?'

We rush down the fifteen flights buzzing with adrenaline until we're back in the basement, holding our sides and desperately trying to catch our breath.

'I can't wait to start digging,' I pant.

'I think there might be something pretty special down there,' says Pria, her cheeks still bright.

'Can't we sit down for a bit first?' Romeo asks, puffing loudly.

Pulling the pallet sofa to one side we make a cosy corner to relax in. With the throws from Romeo's flat, Nani's cushions and other bits and pieces, it's pretty homey. We catch our breath – then Pria asks about the shells.

'Why would someone bury them down here?' she says. 'And how did you manage to figure out the exact spot where they were buried?'

Romeo and I exchange a glance. Then, after a deep breath, I fill Pria in on the whole story. The cat, the objects, the visions – or Nani's memories. My theory about what it all means and how I think I can use the memories to save Nani and show Mum she can cope.

When I'm finished, I'm half expecting Pria to laugh at me but she nods seriously. 'So, you think another memory might be hidden under the shells?'

'Yes. I don't know why but I have a strong feeling I have to dig deeper.'

'*We* have to dig deeper,' Pria corrects, smiling. A warm fuzzy feeling fills me up and I smile back. 'Come on then, let's get to work.'

We stand at the edge of the hole. When I jump into it, the rim of dirt rises to just above my knees.

'Wow,' says Romeo. 'That hole's pretty epic.'

Romeo puts music on a small Bluetooth speaker he brought down and the warmth from the boiler makes us forget the rain outside. He dives into the courtyard and comes back with a rusty old metal shovel, dripping rain on to the floor. 'I saw this the other day.'

'It's an archaeological dig, not an allotment,' I laugh. 'But it definitely means we can make quicker progress.'

The three of us delve further into the soil and scoop it to one side. 'Be careful though, Rome, you might destroy whatever's there.'

He grins. 'Relax!' He does slow down, though.

We all take it in turns to dig down carefully and slowly, until the curve of the hole gets bigger and deeper. The edge of the loose soil is close to my waist now.

Romeo lays the soil on the ground and I sift through with the trowel and my fingers, in case there's anything we missed. But we don't find any more shells, only a woodlouse that scurries over my palms and wriggling worms that poke their tails in the air.

'Fancy some muffins?' asks Pria, leaping out of the hole. 'Mum made them.'

'Great,' I say.

'I brought a flask too,' says Romeo. 'I thought it might be cold today.'

We all sit down on the pallet sofa and Romeo twists off the flask lid and pours us all some steaming hot chocolate.

I wrap my hands around the mug and give Pria a little nod. 'This is nice, isn't it?'

'Yeah,' says Pria. 'And thanks for being here for me – it means a lot.'

Once we've finished our drinks, I nip back upstairs to grab the shoebox with Nani's photos and documents to show Pria and Romeo. We decide that Pria can make a start on the early years of Nani's life once she moved to the tower block when she was twelve.

'I'll use the photos to create a mix of images,' she says, taking her pencil and starting on the blank wall next to the Ghibli figures.

'And me and Xanthe can get on with more digging,' says Romeo, picking up the shovel.

We spend the whole day busy in the den. The rain doesn't give up and we hear it splat against the small windows as we dig further underground, further towards the treasure.

We dig until the hole comes almost up to my shoulders, but still we don't find anything. Could Nani really have buried her memories so deep?

I climb to the side and fling down the trowel. 'Mum'll go spare if she sees these clothes. And all for nothing!'

'I look like I haven't washed for a week,' says Romeo, brushing dirt from his sweatshirt.

I walk across to where Pria's been creating a montage of images. 'The mural's looking fantastic.'

She's sketched the tower block and what the surrounding area used to look like back when Nani moved here. There are rows of terraced houses, the Player's clock tower and a lovely drawing of Nani as a young girl.

'The next step will be to get it all painted,' she says, standing back to look at it properly.

'Shall we call it a day? I think maybe it was just the shells,' says Romeo gently.

'Yeah . . .' I hear my voice fill with disappointment.

'Don't give up yet,' says Pria, staring into the hole. 'We might still find something.' I can't believe how different she is now that she feels part of the group. But I'm not convinced.

'I don't know. Perhaps it *is* just a bunch of old shells.' The excitement I felt last night is fading fast.

'Anyway,' says Romeo, 'if we don't find anything else, I'm sure your nani would still like to see the shells – even that's something.'

'And even without more treasure,' adds Pria, 'you've got plenty of other personal objects to display.'

I give them a lopsided smile and let out a long

sigh. I tell myself to stop being a baby about it, that it doesn't matter. I wanted to find something so badly, something spectacular, but maybe there isn't anything much down here after all.

14

We lock up the den and go with Pria to get her bike.

'Would you like to stay for tea sometime?' I ask her. 'We've got a roof garden. I think you'd love it.'

'Thanks, Xanthe, that would be cool.'

We wave Pria off and watch her splash through the rain, along the cycle path lined with trees.

Back in the flat we eat supper and I collect more information about Nani. We bunch round the table and she tells me how she did well at school and went to Cambridge University and how proud her papa was. I find out how eventually she trained as an archaeologist and I write it all down, but all the time the only thing I can really think about is the stupid failed dig.

*

It's the middle of the night and the cat wakes me from a deep sleep with his insistent mewling. He springs on to my bed and stretches across my head.

He's definitely one hundred per cent a real cat! 'Oi!' I say playfully, as he tugs at my hair.

It's not properly dark and I can see his stripes shimmering in the half-light. I honestly have no clue where this cat's from and after what Mum said about not mentioning it, I guess it'll just have to be our little secret. But Leo seems to think he can come and go as he pleases. Correction – he *is* coming and going whenever he pleases! But for some reason he only likes coming to see me at night.

And as soon as Leo locks me with those blue eyes, I can't wait to see what he's going to show me next. I stretch sleepily and follow the cat as quietly as I can, and this time he leads me up to the roof garden.

A big yellow moon shines down on us as Leo trots between the beds that Mum and Nani have been working on. He jumps along the low wall where Great-grandpa built a small fountain and settles on the place at the back where the water spouts out making soft splashes into the pool.

I always thought cats didn't like water, but this one seems right at home. He begins a thunderous purring and when I look more closely at the blocks of stone Leo is sitting beside, I notice that one of them is different to the others.

Instead of lying flat against the back wall, this stone is missing its pointing and sticks out ever so slightly beyond the main line of stone. Could this be hiding something else Nani concealed when she was younger?

I hurry round to the back of the pool and reach across to prod it lightly with my hand and it wobbles. The stone is one of those rough-cut ones about the size of a postcard and I ease my fingers under the bottom and jiggle it until it moves ever so slightly.

Even though the pointing has crumbled, the stone feels as if it's been firmly wedged in by moss and roots of plants over a long time.

I fetch a small garden fork, prise one of the prongs into a corner of the stone joint and wiggle it back and forth until the stone loosens. When it's far enough forward, I grab the edge and give it a good pull.

All this time Leo doesn't stop purring. It's as if he's egging me on and won't stop until I complete the task.

It's dark in the empty space where the stone sat and when I peer in I can't see much, so I push my hand in and move my fingers around. They knock against something that isn't stone and I curl my fist tight round the object, bringing it into the moonlight.

It's something wrapped in a faded newspaper clipping. I feel myself tremble and a tight feeling clams my chest. I don't know what this is and I'm almost afraid to open it.

In a blur I push the stone back in its slot and take the package over to the dining table. The light from the moon is strong and I don't need to turn on the fairy lights.

I put the package on the table and unfold the newspaper cutting. I glance at the yellowed clipping; it has a photo of an army camp and a headline that reads *Prime Minister Heath Welcomes Ugandan Asians after Expulsion*, but I'm more excited by what's hidden inside.

It's a bronze-coloured bracelet with an inscription along the side.

Still holding the bracelet gently in my palm, I feel the night air turn clammy and hot.

The low whirr of the traffic below turns into the call of insects and loud car horns blast angrily from all directions. When I reach for the edge of the pool to steady myself, I flinch as my hands touch the hot bonnet of a car. I can't see the roof garden any more – only the blinking lights of a vast city spreading away into the night.

And then like a whiplash, in place of the peace, I sense violence, heartache and trouble. I'm not in the garden but in the middle of a street. My heart pounds beneath my ribs – there are army tanks, jeeps and soldiers with guns.

It's night-time and the sky is deepest darkest black. There are no stars or moon. The streets are deserted except for the jeeps and tanks. It looks like a war zone.

A loud siren blares in the background and soldiers with rifles slung across their shoulders stride along the pavements. A soldier stops a car that's driving slowly along the road. I can see the soldier is young. He looks around eighteen or so and the man driving the car is clearly older than him.

In the back of the car, wrapped under a blanket, I can see Maia and the woman from the party day, her mum. The tiny frightened face of a cat with big blue eyes stares out into the darkness.

The soldier makes the man – who must be Maia's dad – get out of the car. He takes a gun from a holster around his waist and prods the tip into the man's chest.

The soldier sounds angry though I can't make out his words. I don't know what the man must have done, but *he doesn't react. He looks at the ground and nods but I can see beads of sweat on his upper lip. The soldier fires the gun, trying to aim for the car tyres, but he misses and the bullet lands beside the car.*

Eventually, the soldier waves the man off. The man doesn't say anything; he picks up the spent bullet from the ground, gets into his car.

They carry on driving. Now I'm in the car too. Maia is screaming and her mum tries her best to console her but she can't stop. The cat is hiding under the back seat, afraid. They keep going slowly through streets filled with more soldiers until they reach the wire fence of an airport.

The family abandons the car and, carrying a small bag each, they walk into the airport crammed already with hundreds of people. The girl has the cat hidden inside her coat.

And then I'm back to the present, in the garden at night with the moon above me. I tug at the edges of my pyjama sleeves, pulling them over my hands. I suddenly feel really cold. Blinking against the darkness and the moon, I shiver.

I have a strong urge to head inside; the shadows in the garden are eerie and this vision has frightened me.

When I get to my room I turn on the lamp, sit up in bed and look at the bracelet carefully. This is no ordinary bracelet. It looks like a bullet casing, hammered flat. I'm sure it's the bullet the soldier in my vision fired, the one Maia's father picked up and put in his pocket.

There's an inscription on the metal:

THIS LAND IS OUR LAND TOO

Etched patterns have been carved around the words, and at either end a fine chain has been attached with a neat clasp.

I try the bracelet on and it fits snugly, as if it was made for someone my size. Even though it's made from a bullet, it's as if it's making a stand against violence and I can see how this could be more powerful than fighting back physically.

15

I lie down in the dark for a while but I can't stop thinking about what happened. I sit up and search for the bracelet on my bedside table. Holding it in my palm I feel the rush of fear I felt in the vision, when the soldier stopped the car. The sound of the gunshot as he fired at the tyre still pounds in my chest.

I've never experienced anything like it and it makes me want to hide deep under my bedclothes, burrow to a place where I feel safe. It's like my insides are all shaken up and I know this wasn't some dream but a real thing which is coming for me, to make me realize that these things are important and that they really happened to Nani in Uganda.

No wonder she's scared to remember.

I can't help wondering what might have happened if things had turned out differently, if the family hadn't got to the airport safely – maybe I wouldn't even have been born.

I read the inscription on the bracelet again – *this land is our land too*. And when she moved into the flats, her dad probably had it made from the bullet . . . but like the flower and shells she must've carried in that small bag at the airport, she hid it away because it was all too painful and upsetting.

I put the bracelet into the special, secret box under my bed, laying it carefully next to the flower and shells, and try to get some sleep.

In the morning I slip out of my room and find Nani in her study, staring at the shelves.

Throwing my arms around her, I give her the biggest hug.

'Hey, you,' she says.

'Shall we do some more of your life story, Nani? Why don't you sit here?' I lead her to the big armchair and collect my notebook, and she begins where we left off before. She tells me what it was like being a student at Cambridge and how she even did some acting when she was there. She tells me about her first job as a young archaeologist and how much she loved it.

After we've been through more photos and I've

made lots more notes, we head to the kitchen where Mum's making brunch.

'The caretaker seems to think that Patrick and Patience next door might be moving.'

'Really?' says Nani. 'Patrick and Patience? They never mentioned anything but then again, they tend to keep themselves to themselves.' Nani frowns. 'I wonder who will move in?'

'Someone nice, I expect,' continues Mum, as she stirs the scrambled eggs.

Once we've finished eating, I hurry my plate into the dishwasher and collect the beautiful box with all the secret, precious things Leo has led me to. I need to show Romeo and Pria the bracelet!

I tiptoe softly to the front door. 'Going round to Romeo's,' I call.

Romeo's mum tells me he's already out and about, so I hurry down the stairwell, and when I get to the den I find Romeo and Pria lounging on the cushions. Now that I understand Pria more, I feel closer to her and don't mind the two of them hanging out – in fact, I'm glad to see her.

'Hey, guys.'

'Hey, Xanthe,' says Pria. 'What've you got there?' She's looking at the box tucked under my arm.

'I brought the things the cat has led me to so far,

so you can both see them. We can start to think about how we'll display everything.'

I lift the lid of the box and we all stare down at the contents. I haven't shared the visions I've had with Pria properly and I'm not sure what she'll think.

'What's the bracelet – you haven't mentioned that before?' Romeo asks.

'I found it last night.' Taking each object, I place them together on a cloth that I spread on the floor. I take a breath, lift the bracelet and hold it so the others can see it clearly. 'It's a bullet!'

Romeo and Pria's eyebrows rise in surprise.

Pria studies it more closely. 'Are you sure?'

I can't help the tears smudging my eyes. 'I saw what happened that night. Great-grandpa drove through streets filled with soldiers and was made to stop. A soldier shot this actual bullet so close to the car, to frighten him. But he picked it up and made this from it.'

Romeo reads the inscription. '*This land is our land too.*'

'We should make sure when we display the bracelet that we surround it with the beauty of Uganda,' says Pria. 'I think that's what those words are telling us. Uganda was your nani's home, and it's not fair she was made to leave.'

I smile, wiping my eyes. 'I agree.'

Pria goes on. 'Even though your nani doesn't have photos, I can find images on the internet.'

'And we can recreate some of Nani's collections too. She had way more than the flower and the shells, but she couldn't bring them with her.'

'I'm OK on the murals,' says Pria, 'but I'm not sure about how to lay the museum out. I haven't really been to many museums.'

'Why don't we take a trip to Wollaton?' Romeo suggests. 'They've got some great displays and we can get some ideas.'

I hold the bracelet carefully in my fingers. Even though I'm not slipping into the vision like before, the horror of that night suddenly feels fresh. Perhaps getting some air would be good. 'Why don't we go now? The sooner we take a look, the quicker we can start planning the display.'

'Let's meet outside in ten minutes,' suggests Romeo. 'Oh, and bring some snacks, Xan – we'll be starving by the time we get there.'

We walk along the busy roads lined with tall plane trees, their bark as mottled as giraffe skin, past the Chinese takeaway and the corner shop with its piles outside of everything you'd ever need. Past the library and the church and the sweetshop where they sell strawberry laces and sherbets in the pick 'n' mix and the barber's where the door is wide open and the street fills with the sounds of music and laughter. We walk until the tower block is left far behind and we're thirsty and hot and the sun is beating on the backs of our necks, making my skin prickle with the heat.

We turn off the main road and take a shortcut to the park. The houses here are big with gardens out front and neatly trimmed hedges. When we pass the final one, Pria pops her head over the gate as if she's looking for something.

'This is my house. Shall we grab a cold drink?' She holds the gate open for us and we throw ourselves on to the cool grass under the shade of a tall tree.

A few minutes later Pria comes back balancing a tray with a plastic jug filled with drink and slices of cucumber. She pours us each an iced glass which we guzzle down in one go.

I peer over to the house with its fancy brickwork and curtains that look like they belong in a theatre, but it's all quiet.

'No one's in,' she says. 'They're both at work.'

'They trust you to look after yourself?' I ask.

'I'm meant to go round to the neighbour's but I

made an excuse and then Mum will be back late afternoon.'

I nod as Pria collects the glasses and takes the tray back.

We carry on to the museum and as soon as we pass the high wrought-iron gates into Wollaton Park we feel like we could be in the countryside, not in the middle of the city.

Through the trees I spy a herd of startled deer running for the shade, the hushed patter of their hooves soft on the grass.

I spot the stately home in the distance, high on the hill. It once belonged to the wealthy Willoughby family, and dates back to the 1500s. We walk up the slope, through the avenue of tall trees and the formal gardens, making our way to the front of the building with the museum inside.

'Let's take some photos of the exhibits,' I say, as we push through the main doors. 'Then we'll have a record for later.'

The doors are stiff and heavy. I like the feel of entering through them – like you have to make an effort to get into the museum with all its ancient history. There's a smell of dust and polish which wraps around us as if it's all part of the experience of being here, and a tang of something like antiseptic reminds me of all the times Nani brought me here and took me to other museums. It's like the memories are exhibits themselves, carefully preserved somewhere in my brain – I take a deep, satisfied breath and resolve to keep them for ever.

'Come on, race you to the avian section.' Romeo whizzes off to find the exhibit we love and visit first every time we come here.

The three of us rush up the sweeping staircase with its smooth wooden banister, turn left at the top, and there they are as always, waiting for us in their wide glass case.

The display is one of the biggest in the museum and it's filled with the most incredible birds.

Among them is a golden eagle with its wings spread wide, a bird of paradise with bright red feathers and our absolute favourite – the shoebill stork with its huge beak like a shovel.

Romeo stares up. 'What have you been up to since we last saw you?'

'It looks like a dinosaur,' says Pria, peering at it from under her lashes like she's not sure about it at all.

'Don't be scared,' I say. 'It's a bit of a shock at first.'

'It does look prehistoric,' says Romeo, studying it

carefully. 'It most likely ate a few small crocodiles in its time.'

'Can you believe this actual one was brought to Europe from Sudan in 1850?' I give Pria a smile.

'I bet it wishes it could fly free like our peregrine though,' says Romeo. 'I'm not sure how I feel about stuffed animals.'

'I agree – we wouldn't do it now, but people would have been amazed to see it back then.'

Pria moves closer to the stork and studies it carefully. 'This is cool. I've not been to many museums before.'

'Not even at school?'

'No, we didn't get to go on many trips. It was just boring old work mostly – not like Mellers. They make everything exciting *and* I'm allowed to paint to help me relax.'

'Yeah.' Romeo shuffles over and gives me a wink. 'It's the best school in the world.'

Even though we're all friends now and neither of them are trying to leave me out, I can't help but feel a pang of jealousy that while they'll be starting Bluecoat secondary school together, I'll be the one going somewhere else alone.

16

'ome on, you guys.' Romeo shoves himself between us. 'Let's get on and go round, or the museum will be closed before we know it.'

Romeo makes a big thing about the fact that I'm the expert in the field and we need to respect that and take note if we're serious about this whole dig and the treasure I've already found.

I give him a grateful smile. Pria seems to have changed her mind about history and listens carefully as we walk around the exhibits. I point out how the entries are written and suggest that we follow the same pattern when we create our own labels for all of Nani's artefacts.

Each section of the museum begins with a large painting giving an artist's impression of that particular time in history.

Pria peers closely at each board.

'You'll be great at that part,' I say, brushing arms with her. 'Maybe you can be in charge of all the artwork, because that's your special talent.'

Pria lights up and her cheeks turn pink. 'Thanks, Xanthe . . . I'd really like that.'

'What's my special talent?' asks Romeo, pretending to be hurt.

'You can be in charge of music, how about that? Maybe do some research into Ugandan music?'

Everyone seems happy with their roles. Time whizzes by and when we get to the final floor, the official in uniform seems to have had enough; he looks bored as he checks his watch and gives a loud yawn.

It must be getting late because the sun streaming through the window bounces against the glass cases and spreads a glow of light across the room.

The official rises from his seat and takes a final slow walk around the exhibits. 'OK, folks, last ten minutes.'

'Well done, everyone,' I say, as we hurry down the stairs. 'We've got lots of photos and now that we've seen how it's done, I think we can get on with creating our very own tower block museum.'

We take a quick selfie beside George the orangutan whose display case has always stood by the entrance.

By the time we leave the museum, most visitors have already left the park, so it's quiet in the grounds. Although it's early evening, the air is still warm and the sun is a flame-red fireball heading towards the horizon.

We walk through the long grass, the scent of summer all around us.

'Look,' I call, 'swallows!'

The air is filled with small dark shapes flying low to the grass, dozens of them, flitting this way and that.

'They love insects,' Romeo says. 'Best time of day – they'll be scooping them up in their beaks, feeding their young and coming back for more.'

Against the gold of the sun, we watch clouds of midges hover above the swishing grass.

'Picnic?' says Romeo, handing round cheese rolls.

We munch on the soft bread and make our way home, out of the high gates of Wollaton Park, past Pria's house where her mum rushes out when we stop by the front wall.

'Darling,' she coos, 'I was worried. Next door said you went to your friend's.' She looks us over and stretches out her hand. 'I'm Pria's mum.'

'We met at the last concert,' says Romeo, shaking her hand so furiously I think it might fall off.

She wrinkles her brow. 'Yes, I remember now. Thanks for keeping my little P company. That's the problem with being an only child, isn't it?'

Pria shuffles about like she wants her mum to stop embarrassing her.

'Wouldn't mind being an only child sometimes,' grins Romeo.

'Shall I drop you off in the car?' asks Pria's mum.

'Thanks,' I reply, 'but we're good. We like walking, don't we, Romeo?'

'Yeah – always more to notice when you're walking.'

We say our goodbyes to Pria and agree to get an early start the next day. Now that we've got lots of inspiration for our tower block museum, I can sense everyone's excitement, and it makes me happy that my idea is starting to take proper shape.

Me and Romeo walk down the wide roads near Pria's house, and continue beside the lanes of busy traffic until we're back at the tower block.

I'm tired by the time I'm at the front door and can't wait to collapse on the sofa. As I slot my key into the lock, I hear noises from the flat.

I close the door behind me and straight away the acrid smell of burning milk hits my nose. 'What's happened? What's that awful smell?'

Mum and Nani are in the kitchen and they both have blotchy faces and red eyes. The windows are wide open but there's not much of a breeze and the smell hangs in the air.

'It's all my fault,' cries Nani. 'I thought I'd turned the pan off but I went for a nap.'

Mum's worry grooves are really deep. 'By the time I came down from the garden the pan was burnt beyond repair.' She lowers her eyes. 'Imagine if I wasn't here. Nani was asleep. There could have been a fire.' This isn't like Mum – she's usually the calm one, but this has really put her on edge.

I fiddle with the sleeve of my sweatshirt, worry knots pulling at my belly. 'Are you OK, Nani?' I'm not sure what I can say to make any of this better.

'No, Xanthe, I'm not OK.' Nani is trembling, her hand shaking like a fluttering leaf.

I put my arm around her. 'Don't worry. We've got this, haven't we, Mum?'

Mum doesn't reply; she's just staring at the burnt pan.

'I'll make us all a cup of tea,' I say. I try hard to keep my tears from falling, as they're not going to help anyone. Over by the sink the blackened milk pan is unrecognizable and the hob is still covered in thick charred lumps.

I fill the kettle and switch it on and once it's boiled I bring the mugs over to the table. 'Mum, let's go into the sitting room.'

She's staring blankly, but takes Nani by the elbow and guides her away from the stink of the kitchen. I close the door firmly and spray some air freshener around. Things are even more serious than I thought.

Later, once we've thrown the milk pan in the big bins outside and scrubbed the kitchen down, I think things are starting to settle down. But when I go to the bathroom I hear Mum on the phone in her bedroom and I hear the muffled words *Treetops Lodge*.

The care home!

I sneak closer to the door, which is shut, making her words a low whisper. I press my ear right up against it but she's talking quietly.

I hear snatches . . . *fire*, *dangerous*, *lives alone*.

A sad feeling winds its way to the pit of my belly and begins to churn. Mum's obviously worried about Nani and considering the care home again.

Just when we were starting to think of making a special surprise for Nani to heal her, Mum's got ideas of her own.

My ear's right up against the keyhole now, and that's the only way I hear the word *tomorrow*.

Tomorrow. Tomorrow what? Then, suddenly, I know exactly what she means. Nani will be going to the home *tomorrow*!

I won't let this happen. Whatever the situation, there has to be something I can do.

'How are you feeling, Nani?' I sit beside her in the living room and take her hand. All the emotions from snooping on Mum's call are swirling inside me and I feel like I could cry – but I don't.

'I feel such a fool.' Her lip trembles.

'It's not your fault.'

'I – I keep thinking . . . what if your mum hadn't been here? I was fast asleep, Xanthe. I didn't smell anything.'

'I know, Nani – but she *was* here and it's sorted now.'

'But she can't always be here. I've been trying to jolly myself along, but the truth is I know I'm making mistakes, forgetting things – next time it could be something even worse.'

Mum opens the door. 'Your dad's coming to stay later tonight,' she says to me. 'Isn't that nice?' Her eyes are red but she manages a watery smile, which I don't return.

17

I've nearly fallen asleep when I hear the quiet click of the front door and Dad's voice out on the landing.

When he comes into the room, I keep my eyes pressed closed as he plants a kiss on my head. I don't trust myself to stay quiet if he asks how I am, so I turn to face the wall and he tiptoes away.

This might be the last time I sleep here, in Mum's old room – it might be the last time I take Nani a cup of tea in the morning. Unless I do something, tomorrow she'll be at Treetops Lodge with a bunch of strangers who don't know her and won't understand about her past, her home, and what it means to her.

The rooftop garden will get pulled down and all those years of tending and growing will disappear in the blink of an eye as if it had never been here.

I don't think I can bear it – I feel so connected to Nani, especially when I'm here. I love the thought that Great-grandpa left his mark on everything he touched and cared for. It's like he's still here in each flower that blooms and every time a new leaf shoots out.

It's my past too and helps me know who I really am and what came before.

All through the night, dreams of who might live in the flat burst into my head. I see a sad-faced Nani sitting by a lonely window waiting for us to visit. I just can't let it happen – I *won't* let it happen!

In the morning I hear someone shuffling about in the bathroom, twisting the noisy taps, and Mum's voice talking in hushed whispers.

All at once, the realization hits me. It's *tomorrow* and all my worst fears are coming true.

I have to do something!

Hands shaking, I hurriedly text Pria and Romeo and tell them we need to meet up ASAP.

But before I try anything else, I should probably try talking to my parents.

The bathroom door bangs and Dad's heavy foot-steps thud over to my room. I quickly jump back as he twists the knob and pops his head in.

'You were asleep when I came last night.' He

comes over and gives me a cuddle. 'I've missed you.'

'Missed you too.' I snuggle closer, creasing his freshly ironed shirt.

'I've got to go now, but I'll be back this evening. Your mum needs my help.'

I grab hold of his hand. 'What with?'

His face flushes red like he's trying to hide something. He's always been a rubbish liar. 'N-nothing.'

'Dad,' I hiss. 'I know there's something going on.'

'Look, I'm going to be late for work.'

I lower my voice. 'It's to do with Nani, isn't it?'

He shifts his eyes everywhere but in my direction, which confirms my suspicions. 'We'll talk to you about it soon – but don't mention *anything* to your mum. Later.'

He blows me a kiss as he hurries out of my room, and a few moments later shuts the front door.

When I go to the kitchen, Mum's busy chopping vegetables for soup.

'I know you and Dad have been talking,' I say, 'about what to do with Nani.'

'Not now, Xanthe.'

'Why won't you tell me what's going on?'

Mum ignores me and continues to furiously chop the onions.

'I'm part of the family too. You can't just keep everything a secret. I know what's going on.'

'I said not now – it's all too complicated.'

I stomp back into my room and throw myself on the bed. Everything I suspected is true and my parents won't even admit it – so how am I supposed to persuade them to change their minds?

Nani's moving to Treetops, the flat will get sold and someone else will move in. After all these years the family home with all its memories will disappear. The home that Great-grandpa fought so hard to buy after arriving here with only £50 will become a forgotten dream for Nani.

I bite my lip – and I can't even rage at Mum and make her change her mind, because clearly Nani doesn't know anything about this yet: they're keeping it all from her as well as me, and I don't want to worry her by causing an argument.

I bang angry fists against the covers, tears making a damp mess of the duvet. If I can't talk to Mum and Dad, I'll see what the gang have to say. Perhaps together we can come up with a plan.

Once Romeo and Pria arrive, I hurry them into my room. We sit on my bed and I tell them in a hushed voice about everything that's happened, all about the milk boiling over, the leaflets and how Mum's planning on sending Nani to a care home.

I'm barely finished when Mum knocks on the door and we fall silent. She's carrying a tray of juice and cookies.

'I thought you might like some snacks,' she says, setting down the tray on the bedside table. She searches our wide eyes and tight lips. 'What are you all so quiet for?'

'Um, no reason,' I blurt.

But Mum clearly doesn't have the energy to question me. 'Xanthe, me and Nani have got to nip out around four-ish for an appointment,' she says casually. 'But let's not tell her until it's time to go, OK? I don't want her to worry – she gets so anxious about these appointments.' My tummy somersaults. This must be when she's taking Nani to Treetops Lodge! Mum's talking to Romeo and Pria now. 'You can stay for lunch if you like. I've checked with your parents.'

'Cool,' says Pria.

'That would be awesome,' says Romeo.

When the door closes behind Mum, I let out a squashed-up breath. 'Four o'clock – that's when Mum's going to take Nani to the old people's home!' I feel my belly clench. 'This is just not fair. This flat

140

is her home – and I feel like the memory museum could really help her! Now we won't have time to finish it before it's too late.'

Romeo brushes his arm against mine and gives me a crooked smile. 'Don't worry, we'll think of something.'

'This happened to someone *my* gran knows.' Pria flicks me a sympathetic glance and hands me the plate of cookies. 'It was really upsetting.'

'Sometimes she's fine and other times she gets really confused. And how could they not even discuss it with me.' I feel the anger from earlier heat my cheeks. I pick up a cookie even though I don't have any appetite. 'They're keeping everything from me so I can't even say what I feel.'

'Why can't you just challenge them?' asks Pria.

'They're being so secretive. Dad said not to mention it and I know with everything going on Nani will get really upset if we all start arguing.'

Pria's face lights up. 'What if we dropped your nani off at mine for a bit this afternoon, when she's supposed to be at her appointment? If she's not in the flat your mum can't take her anywhere.'

'How would I persuade Nani, though? She'll think it's really weird.'

Romeo narrows his eyes like he's trying to think

of a way. 'You could tell her you want to go to the museum again?'

'Yeah – I could tell her I've already cleared it with Mum,' I add. 'But doesn't the museum close at four? I feel like we might have to keep her occupied longer to make sure Mum can't take her to the home.'

'Yes,' says Pria, 'but then after the museum I'll suggest we watch a film at my house, which is right nearby. And then once the film's over it'll be too late to go to the home for sure.'

It sounds like a bit of a ropey plan but I can't think of a better one so I nod.

'She wouldn't need to stay away for ever,' says Romeo. 'Just until your parents take notice of you. And listen to you.'

'Mum'll be worried.'

'Romeo's right,' says Pria. 'They'll be worried but it'll make them listen to you and take you seriously after that. I mean, if you can actually kidnap your own gran, they'll wonder what else you're prepared to do to stop them.'

I begin to get fired up now. 'It'll definitely get their attention. And you're sure your mum will be OK with it?'

'I'll text her now.' Pria taps away at her phone and a message pings back straight away. 'Yeah, no probs

– she'll enjoy having your nan over. It's probably just the distraction she needs.'

I suddenly feel better about Nani. At least this way I'll be with her all the time so she won't worry, and it will show Mum and Dad how strong my feelings are. *And* I'll be doing something about it rather than just fretting.

We've polished off our juice and snacks when a sudden crashing and banging from next door makes us all jump.

As we go into the hallway, Nani peers out of the living room. She looks really worried. 'What's going on?'

'I don't know, Nani.' I take her hand and lead her to a chair.

'They're probably just moving furniture, Mrs B,' says Romeo.

Mum wanders out of the kitchen and opens the front door. 'I think next door really *are* moving,' she says, shutting the door when she's had a good look. 'There's a huge lorry waiting outside and the entrance is jammed with boxes.'

Nani looks worried again.

'I'm sure it will be someone nice moving in,' Mum says breezily, though she looks a bit frazzled. I can tell she's trying hard to sound chilled about it, but underneath she's probably as upset as Nani – another change to get used to.

'Anyway, we're treating this lot to a barbie lunch on the roof, aren't we?' says Mum. 'I think we can all do with cheering up. Mum, do you want to start making a tomato salad? Xanthe, Pria, Romeo, perhaps you can help me bring up the plates and things?'

I put music on to take my mind off the plan for the moment. I can't let Mum suspect anything.

Before long we're carrying drinks and snacks up to the roof garden and have forgotten about next door for the minute.

When we get out into the fresh air everything feels better. Mum lights the barbecue and we all gather round the table with our drinks.

I notice a few weeds have sprung up between the bean plants and I crouch close to the soil and begin pulling them out. Romeo joins me and together we clear the fresh patch of dandelions and drop them on the compost pile.

'This is amazing.' Pria takes her glass and walks through the garden, her eyebrows rising like surprised half-moons. We give Pria a tour of the borders, the lush planting of summer vegetables and herbs, the wide-leafed bananas with tiny rows of yellow fruits sitting snugly next to each other.

I pick a bunch of holy basil to sprinkle on the tomato salad and Romeo sneaks a ripe pod of peas and pops it open.

'These are incredible,' he says, dropping them into his mouth.

'Nani's papa started the garden when they moved from Uganda; back then for some reason the flat came with this outdoor space.'

'Yeah, your family are lucky – none of the other top flats are allowed the roof.'

'He put so much love and care into it and passed it on to Nani. And,' I lower my voice to a whisper, 'I don't think she could bear it if she had to leave.' My eyes feel damp. 'If that happens all this will go to ruin.'

The others make a tight circle around me.

'It won't come to that,' says Pria, kicking at the ground. 'We've got a plan.'

'Thanks, Pria.'

Romeo suddenly shoots away from us towards the edge of the garden, where the trellis forms a high barrier hiding the drop to the streets below. 'It's the peregrine!' he shouts, pointing towards the tower block opposite.

We shuffle in beside him and strain our eyes to the spot where he's looking.

'I can't see anything.' Pria concentrates hard in the direction of the other tower block.

'There,' breathes Romeo, as if the falcon will hear us and startle.

I follow his finger to the very edge of the other tower block, find the outcrop of ledge and see a blob of grey. 'How do you know it's the peregrine?'

'I've been observing it from my room – through my binoculars – and I looked it up on the internet. It's just like the photo online.'

'I've seen it from my window too – but I wasn't sure what it was.'

'Wait, it's getting ready to fly.'

I hold my breath.

We watch the bird lift its sharp wings, rise from the tower block into the blue sky and zoom like a comet across the open space between us.

It feels so thrilling to see this magnificent bird full of power and speed, and yet it's here and not in some far-off wilderness as you might expect.

It's just like Nani has always said, there's so much right under our noses, it's here for everyone, we only need to take notice.

I'm suddenly reminded that I haven't seen Leo the cat for a while and wonder whether he's found a place that's easier to get into with better snacks. And how did he know where to find all the things Nani hid when she was little?

I remember the cat Nani was holding under her coat, in the last memory. And the cat in the tree, during the previous memory with the flower. Did they look similar to Leo? Looking back, it's hard to tell.

We return to the table where Nani is making sure we all have enough food on our plates. Mum finishes off dishing out the grilled chicken, then nips downstairs to fetch some ketchup. While she's out of earshot, I decide to ask Nani about Leo.

'Nani, you know you said you had a cat in Uganda, can you tell us what it was like?'

Nani frowns like she's trying to catch the memory of him. 'He was such a handsome cat – a Bengal. He was much bigger than regular house cats.'

'Was he really special?'

Nani smiles. 'He *was* special, but mainly because he was *my* cat. Papa brought him home one day from a rescue centre and I thought he'd brought me a tiger. He had dark fur with the most incredible striped markings. He was cute as a button with his enormous blue eyes.'

My own eyes widen. A big striped cat with blue eyes? Surely . . .

'What was he called?' asks Romeo, picking up on where I'm heading with my line of questioning.

'Leo.' She pauses. 'He was called Leo.'

I feel a jolt. Leo. That's what was written on the name-tag of the cat I've seen.

But that's not possible: Nani's Leo would have been gone for decades.

Then again . . . how would a cat know where Nani hid all of her memories, anyway?

18

It's three by the time we finish lunch on the roof garden. I'm buzzing with excitement and nerves about the plan to save Nani.

Romeo and Pria say goodbye and make their way downstairs to wait as arranged. A little while after, I tell Mum – who's stacking the dishwasher – I'm taking Nani out for a quick walk.

When she's not looking, I sneak Nani's phone out of her bag and leave it in her room.

I've told Nani we're going to the museum so she knows what's happening and she thinks I've told Mum.

Mum's sitting in the kitchen with a big mug of tea. She's got dark circles under her eyes and I feel a sudden pang of guilt.

'Have a lovely walk.' She helps Nani with her jacket and gives her a peck on the cheek. When

Nani's safely out of earshot in the hall, Mum reminds me to be home by four.

I feel my palms slick with sweat, as I imagine her peering out of the window to see if she can spot us. When it starts to get late, she'll call Dad.

But I push those feelings away. It won't be for long and Nani won't be in any danger.

I turn quickly to face the door. 'See you later, Mum.'

'Have a nice relax, love,' says Nani, following me out.

We take the lift to the ground floor where the gang are waiting at the entrance.

Nani gives a smile. 'This is going to be fun – a bit of an adventure. I haven't been to the museum in ages.'

We walk out of the tower block and past the play park and the mums and dads pushing toddlers on the swings. I look up towards Nani's flat, imagine Mum still in the kitchen, enjoying the silence and not having to think about Nani for a while. I hook my arm in Nani's and we chit-chat away. I forget about Mum and concentrate on the plan.

We continue past the clump of trees, along the street with its line of shops: the newsagent's where I get Nani's paper, the greengrocer's with its neatly stacked boxes of yellow mangoes that make my mouth water and the bakery where the window is heaving with pastries piled one on top of the other.

The smell of frying fish from the takeaway drifts out and teases our taste buds.

After about half an hour of walking, we arrive at the museum. Nani loves it and can't believe she hasn't been here for so long. She chats with the guides about her work as an archaeologist and is the most relaxed and happy I've seen her for ages. Still, I stay close by in case she needs any help, but once she's talking about the subject she loves best, she grows in confidence.

I check my watch. It's nearly four so we hurry through the final rooms and make our way outside.

Nani's face is flushed with the excitement of the museum visit and it all feels so good, except there's a small knot that pings from time to time as I imagine Mum expecting us back any moment.

'I wondered if we could stop by my house and watch a film?' Pria suggests, as planned. 'I live just there.'

Nani is delighted. 'That sounds great – if your parents don't mind? I could do with a sit-down.'

'Of course not,' Pria says. 'Mum's home and she'd love to meet you.'

I glance at my phone and it's five past four – we're officially late now and there's already a message from Mum. I turn off my phone without reading it.

We're at Pria's house in no time. 'Welcome,' says Pria, swinging open the gate and leading the way down the path to the blue front door. She knocks before opening it up with her keys.

Pria's mum is already in the hallway.

'I'm Pearl,' she says, wiping her wet hands on her apron before holding out a hand to Nani. 'Pleased to meet you. I've got everything ready for the film. I think it's really cute. Pria doesn't get to see her granny too much since she lives in Singapore and I know she's really enjoyed hanging out with you. Anyway, listen to me chattering away – come in, come in.' She gives Pria a cuddle.

We all pile into the sitting room and flop on the squashy sofas while her mum heads to the kitchen. It's a big sunny room with a piano at one end and French doors that open on to the flowery garden at the other.

'Can I?' asks Romeo, sitting down at the piano.

'Sure,' says Pria. 'My dad plays, so I think it's tuned and everything.'

Romeo begins a classical piece and Pria's mum brings the tea things in. She pours steaming tea into cups for her and Nani. 'Beautiful playing, Romeo – there's squash for you all too.'

'So far so good,' I whisper to Pria, slurping my blackcurrant drink.

Pria gives me a reassuring smile, then turns on the TV and scrolls through a streaming service. 'What shall we watch? I already saved some of my favourites.'

There are some Studio Ghibli movies, obviously, but several comedies too.

'What about this?' Nani points out *Night at the Museum*.

'Sounds good, Mrs B!' says Romeo.

'Yeah, cool,' agrees Pria.

'Very on-brand,' I say, hugging Nani tightly.

I know I should check my phone – it's half past four now, and Mum will be worried – but instead I stow it in my rucksack. Out of sight, out of mind.

After the movie, the evening is still light and the summer sun is glinting across the lawn into the sitting room. I think the walk and looking at the exhibits tired Nani out because halfway through the movie she fell asleep on the sofa.

I check my watch and the blue numbers light up – 19:45. I feel my stomach twist. I bet Mum's left a hundred messages on my phone but I can't bear to look.

Pria helps her mum bring trays of food into the garden and I wake Nani up gently. She takes a few minutes to sort herself out before we go and sit at the table.

'Thank you, dear,' says Nani to Pria's mum, blinking awake. 'This is so kind of you.'

We bite into the veggie burgers and home-made coleslaw and suddenly with all the worrying and walking I feel ravenous and shovel down the food.

Nani pats her pocket. 'Now where did I put that phone?'

I clear my throat and give the others a sly glance. 'I saw it on the hallway table before we left, but I put it away safely in your room.'

Nani smiles. 'Thanks, love – I don't think I'll need it anyway. It's just habit. I'm always losing it!'

'Me too,' laughs Pria's mum. 'I'm forever having to call it up to find where I've put it.'

If it weren't for thinking about Mum, I'd be feeling really relaxed and happy like Nani is, but I know at some point I have to turn on my phone and check the messages.

We sip fizzy iced lemonade through paper straws and Pearl has skewered strawberries and dunked

154

them in too, like fun mocktails.

'I think I'd better look at my phone,' I say in a whisper.

'I think you should,' says Pria. 'You've already done what you set out to do – it'll be far too late for them to go to the home now.'

'You'll have to face the music at some point,' agrees Romeo, taking a bite of burger. He digs his phone from his pocket and flashes it at me. There's a line of messages from his mum and they all say: *Where are you?* or *Are you with Xanthe?*

'What are you lot whispering about?' Pria's mum comes over and refills our glasses.

'Nothing,' says Pria, looking at the floor.

The sky is turning a beautiful deep blue like it does on the best summer evenings and birds are singing their night-time lullabies. Nani starts to talk about going home.

I take my phone from my rucksack and walk towards the trees at the bottom of the garden.

As I step into the shade of the trees and turn the phone on, my heart flies to my mouth. Just as I thought, hundreds of messages flood the screen.

19

The phone messages light up my screen:

Where are you?

What's happened?

Is Nani OK?

Have you had an accident?

Call me!!!!

Xanthe – WHERE ARE YOU!!!

I'd like to turn my phone off again and throw it into the long grass beyond the trees, but I know it's time to accept the consequences of what I've done – and hope that it's worth it.

I hover over the red *stop the call* button, but before I can bring my finger down, Mum picks up.

'Is everything OK?' Mum is teary, and instead of sounding angry, she just sounds really worried.

'Mum?'

'Something bad's happened, hasn't it?'

I lean against the fence. 'Mum, listen – everything's OK. Nani's fine.' I take a deep breath before Mum can process any of this, and dive in. 'I don't want her to move to Treetops Lodge.' I feel hot tears slide down my face. 'I want us to look after Nani. I thought if I did something dramatic, you'd have to listen.'

There's silence on the other end of the phone and I can hear Dad's voice in the background.

'Your mum's been worried sick.' Dad's taken the phone and he sounds really stressed. 'Where *are* you?'

'We're not coming back until you promise not to send Nani to a care home.'

'Xanthe, listen to me. It's really important that you come back. Nani needs her medicines and she needs familiarity.' I can see him now, pushing his hand through his hair, getting all agitated.

'Actually, Nani's fine and we're having a fun time.' The hard lump in my throat is aching and I try to keep my voice steady. 'We're at Pria's house. Romeo's parents know where it is.'

I quickly turn the phone off before he can say any more. At least they know we're safe now. Walking back slowly up the curving path, I kick at the loose stones.

'Is everything OK, Xanthe?' Nani stares at my blotchy face.

'Mmmm – yes. I just called Mum to let her know we're all fine.'

'She does worry a lot.' Nani takes my hand. 'Come on, Pearl's made an Eton Mess for pudding.'

Pria and Romeo raise their eyebrows at me and I give them a weak smile. But before we've even lifted our spoons to dig into the raspberry meringue and cream, there's the screech of a car arriving outside. Doors slam, the gate clicks open and Mum and Dad rush into Pria's garden and push the bell frantically.

'What?' Nani is the first to speak.

'I'm guessing you're Xanthe's mum and dad?' says Pearl, letting them in. 'Come and join us for pud . . .' She trails off, because neither of their faces look like they want to stay for pudding. 'Is something wrong?' she asks.

Dad clears his throat. 'I'm sorry everyone, but Xanthe and Maia need to get home.' He stabs his eyes at me. 'We have a bit of an emergency back at the flat.'

The gang send me sympathetic glances.

'Oh dear,' says Nani. 'It's not the hob again, is it? Or did I leave the bath running?' Her face crumples.

Mum comes round and puts her hands on Nani's shoulders. 'No, Mum, nothing like that – but we just need to get home.'

All the way back in the car Mum and Dad are quiet but I expect once we get inside they'll let rip.

Nani chats away, which is a relief, telling them all about the evening and how kind Pearl is and how she made the most lovely pudding, if only they could have had time to try it.

Once the flat door is firmly closed and Nani is snoozing in the living room, I wait for the row to begin.

Worry sits like a block of ice in the pit of my belly as Mum, Dad and I go into the kitchen and sit around the table.

'Xanthe, we understand why you did what you did today. But you know it was wrong, don't you?' Mum's eyes are swimming with tears and Dad squeezes her hand.

'We didn't know where you or Nani were – for hours,' Dad adds. 'We were starting to think about calling the police.'

Suddenly I feel like crying too. I nod. I managed to get their attention but I really worried them in the process. 'I'm sorry,' I murmur. 'I just really don't want you to put Nani in a home.'

Mum studies me. 'Xanthe – your nani really isn't well, there's no point in denying it.' She pauses. 'We're going to have to keep all our options open. For the future. Do you understand?'

I don't reply. Tears are spilling over my cheeks.

Now Dad takes over. 'We know this is painful, it's painful for us too – but we need you to be grown-up about this and strong. Nani may not need to live in a care home for years yet, but that time may come – if her needs become greater than what we all want or can do.'

It's not what I wanted to hear and I feel like closing my ears off to all of it. My plan hasn't worked – I've just delayed the inevitable. The museum and Nani's repressed memories are even more important now – because unless I show Mum and Dad that Nani can get better, she'll still end up going into the home. I can't let that happen.

All the things the cat has led me to are important – I know it. Nani has to face her past in order to heal.

When I go to my room I close the door firmly behind me. I startle as I notice a shimmer-shape stretching out on my bed – it's Leo! As if thinking about him earlier has made him magically appear.

'Where have you been? I haven't seen you for a

while. And I'm not following you anywhere either,' I whisper.

Leo appears to understand because he doesn't try to lead me out of my room. Instead, tiredness and sadness turn my limbs floppy as I struggle into my pyjamas, and he simply watches, slow-blinking. I slip under the covers and draw them tight to my chin. Leo rests his head on my chest and I watch it rise and fall with each sleepy breath. Perhaps he just knew I needed a hug.

I'm flitting in and out of dreams when I feel Leo move to the foot of the bed. When I open my eyes to see what he's up to, the cat has disappeared.

20

'We have to get on with the museum,' I say next morning, looking at the half-finished paintings on the basement walls. After yesterday's conversation with Mum and Dad, I'm bursting with purpose.

'We'll have to work out how to display the objects,' says Romeo, leaning back on the cushions.

I've already told them what happened after I got home, so they know this is even more important now. There's a real energy and urgency in the den.

'We could build some shelves for them,' suggests Pria. 'Like we saw at Wollaton.'

'My dad's got lots of bits and pieces in his work-shop down in the garages,' says Romeo, jumping up. 'He might let us have some.'

'Great – what if you take charge of that part? I'll do the writing and Pria, you could carry on with the paintings?'

We spend the next few days furiously toing and froing between the flat, the den and Romeo's dad's workshop.

Whenever I'm back in the flat, I hear Mum and Dad whispering to each other in the kitchen. I know they're discussing Treetops Lodge and I'm even more determined to finish the museum before it's too late.

Nani and I hang out in the evenings, talking about her memories of growing up here in the tower block – but all the while, in my mind, I'm seeing Uganda and wondering if and how it will heal her.

At last, the museum is just about finished and we all agree that it's absolutely amazing.

Now we just have to get Nani down here and see what happens.

In the middle of the night a scratching sound on my door wakes me up.

'It's you!' I hiss. I eye the cat suspiciously. 'Where did you get to the other night? You disappeared right in front of my eyes.' I pause. 'I keep wondering if you're the same cat Nani had when she was little, somehow.'

The cat blinks at me as if to say, 'So what?'

I open the door wider but Leo doesn't want to come in. He flashes his electric-blue eyes at me and turns his head away.

'It's the following game, is it? Are you leading me to another of Nani's memories?' Suddenly wide awake, I grab my dressing gown and traipse after him all the way down the ghostly-quiet stairwell, his shimmery glow leading me into the den where the low hum of the boiler is like a snoring dragon.

In the half-light the paintings look amazing spread out across the walls. Leo's stripes glimmer as he pads over to the discarded hole where I found the shells.

'Not this again,' I mumble.

But he ignores me completely and stands beside the hole that we've left open, though roped off with string – like a real archaeological exhibition, where they show where things were found.

The orange blur of a street light stretches across the floor. A shiver ripples down my spine as I flick a look around the spooky den. Leo dives into the hole and disappears. 'Oh, Leo . . . there's nothing else there. We already looked, remember? I'm going to bed.'

I turn to leave but he pounces in front of me quick as light and leads me back to the gaping hole.

'OK.' I yawn and shrug off my dressing gown. 'But I'm not spending ages on this wild goose chase of yours.'

He hovers by the hole, lifts his face to mine, his blue eyes gripping me, forcing me to look.

When I stare past the cat, something in the hole catches my eye. It shines in the orange light, and I think I see the tiniest corner of something poking out.

How didn't we notice it before? There *is* something else in there! Some memory Nani buried before the shells – maybe before anything else. It could be the most important memory of all.

I jump into the hole, find the bright scrap of whatever it is and brush away the soil around it with my fingers, but it's buried much deeper and the earth is compacted around it.

Nerves like ants crawl across my insides as I hurriedly find the trowel and begin digging close to the buried object, loosening the dirt.

Shakily scrambling on to my hands and knees, I keep digging away for maybe half an hour until slowly from under the soil I uncover something – a gold-painted tin.

'Leo! You genius!' My heart is thrumming loudly and in the soft orange light it feels almost like a dream. But when I lean forward and place my palms on its flat surface, it's cold and definitely real.

The tin is round, about the size of a hatbox with a brass fastening. Lots of the paint has chipped away and it's old and dirty.

I lift the box out of the hole, put it on the side and use the brush to clean some of the earth away.

'I need to get this upstairs to take a closer look.' My chest feels tight and fizzy and a happy feeling springs all over my body as I hold it tight. But no memories spring to life – not yet. If there is a memory, it's probably inside the box.

I remember the feeling I had when I first arrived at Nani's, as I lay on the grass, imagining all the roots winding down, curling around pocketfuls of dark earth, guarding secrets.

Part of me wants to fling open the lid straight away but I have to control myself and do this properly.

My heart tap-taps against my ribs.

Leo winks a blue eye at me. I turn for a second to examine the tin and when I look back . . . what a surprise: he's gone!

Carrying the tin carefully, I go back to the flat. But once I'm by our front door I think of Romeo asleep on the other side of the wall and suddenly want to share this incredible find with him.

I slip inside, grab my phone and text him:

Meet me in the roof garden –
I'll leave the door on the latch
Exciting development!!!
??????

Heading silently up to the roof garden, I place the round yellow tin on the table and turn on the fairy lights. I take a breath of cool night air, damp and fresh. Romeo might not wake up and I know his mum usually bans phones from bedrooms, but fingers crossed he sneaked it in anyway.

Just when I think he's not coming, the door shushes open.

'Over here,' I whisper.

'What is it?' He stumbles over and groggily sits beside me. He's still dozy and rubs at his eyes.

The magic of the night wraps itself around us and I nod at the tin.

'A discovery,' I smile. 'Night-digging in the den!'

'What?'

'It was that cat. He woke me up and insisted we go to the den – and I found this! I haven't opened it or anything because I wanted us to do it straight away and together, that's why I wanted you to come.'

I place my hands on the tin again and it's as if I

can feel an energy coming from it, a buzzing tingling at my fingers, the same as each of the other times Leo has led me to a treasure.

The brass catch is delicate and finely made. 'Shall we do it?'

Romeo nods.

I flip the fastening open, hands shaking, and ceremoniously lift the lid.

'Wow,' says Romeo.

Butterflies flit about my belly like they're doing a victory dance.

'Double wow!' I breathe. 'It's incredible.'

21

Inside the yellow tin there's a sort of crown. It's made with long feathers. Some of them are milk white and others are bright blue. A little red one is neatly tucked to one side and they're all fixed to an intricate gold band. Me and Romeo stare mesmerized into the tin. I feel my heart thrum against my chest, blood pumping loudly in my ears.

'See! I knew there'd be something magnificent down there and that eventually we'd find it.'

'You were right all along, Xan – this really is treasure. Do you think we should lift it out to get a better look?'

'OK, but we have to be careful. We mustn't damage it.' I'm feeling really protective over the crown, as if I was meant to find it and I'm its guardian.

The sky has cleared and the clouds are rimmed

with the pale peach light of dawn. A single lonely star shines down on us and our treasure.

We stare at the crown like we can't believe we actually found something and I know exactly how all those archaeologists felt the moment they knew they'd found important pieces from the past. Now that it's bathed in light, I can see that it must once have had stones to decorate it. There are claws of fine hammered metal that probably held the precious gemstones – ten empty spaces along the gold band.

'Looks like it's missing the most valuable part,' says Romeo, noticing the same thing.

'That's a shame. I bet it was even more beautiful when it was complete.' I pause. 'I wonder why Nani buried this.'

'Do you think you'll find out . . . if you touch it?' Romeo suggests.

I take a deep breath. Then I reach out, lift the crown and place it on my head.

The wall of the roof garden is shifting, changing from solid concrete, becoming the thick trunk of a tree. I press my back against its smooth bark. I blink up into the canopy, where white fluffy clouds peek through the lacy leaves. The ground of the garden has turned to roughly knotted planks as I realize I'm on a verandah, standing between a house and a tropical garden filled with birdsong.

I feel a ripple pass through my body and I'm in that other world again. Uganda. My nani's childhood. I see the big beautiful trees I saw before and panic grips my lungs. What terrible thing's going to happen this time? But there's nothing I can do to stop this and I tumble into the vision.

Out on the verandah the family are gathered around the table. The man takes a stack of blue passports bound by an elastic band and puts them in the inside pocket of his jacket. There are suitcases in one corner and bundles wrapped in bright fabric in another.

The birds are singing but the atmosphere is tense. The family doesn't say much and when I look closely at their faces they're streaked with tears.

Nani has a cat snuggled under her arm, purring loudly, and she strokes it gently. I peer at it. The markings on its body, its eyes and even the tag around its neck are identical to Leo's.

'Maia,' a voice calls from inside the house.

Nani runs inside, to the kitchen, and the cat follows her with the speed of a cheetah. Maia jumps into the open arms of a young woman, the one I've seen before. Maia buries her face into her shoulder and cries – loud, frantic, inconsolable sobs.

'Come on,' says the young woman, peeling Maia's fingers from her own. 'I have something to show you.' She leads her up the sweeping staircase with its polished wooden banister and they go into the little girl's bedroom.

On the centre of her bed I spot the feather crown, but this one has dark red gemstones set into it.

'Mercy!' the little girl cries. 'What is this? Are these the rubies we found?' Her eyes are full of wonder as she lifts the crown reverently. 'It's so beautiful.' Maia squeezes Mercy's hand. 'And you even put my lucky red feather in.'

'It's a magic crown,' Mercy says quietly, sitting down beside Maia.

Maia's eyes are wide. 'This is magic?'

'That's right.' Mercy gently clasps Maia's hand. 'Whenever you wear it, see, you'll remember me. You'll remember all of this – your home. Try it on.'

Mercy places it on Maia's head, the polished metal shining, the feathers bright and the rubies glinting in the sunlight, brilliant against her dark hair. But tears are running down her cheeks.

'I don't want to have to remember you. Mercy, why can't you come too?'

'Hush,' soothes the young woman. 'I can't come.' She's trying to help Maia be brave but I can see that her gentle eyes are brimming with tears too.

Maia removes the crown from her head. 'But I can't bring the crown anyway,' she says. 'The rubies are too valuable. Papa says we can't bring anything of worth or they'll take it from us.'

Mercy's eyes lower in disappointment – she obviously hadn't considered this. Then she swipes her tears away and holds Maia's hands in her own.

'So we do what we have to do.' She brings out a small penknife from her pocket and flicks it open. 'If we take out the rubies they won't be interested in the crown. I promise the magic will still work without them.'

Carefully and slowly Mercy digs the tip of the penknife into the metal and levers them out one by one.

Maia rushes to a drawer, pulls out a scarf and lays it on the tabletop.

Mercy flicks a glance towards the window and places the ten large rubies on the scarf, folds it neatly and puts it in her pocket. 'We will see each other again. When this is all over, you'll come back and we'll reunite the magic crown with its rubies. I promise.'

She folds Maia in the biggest embrace and I watch until the image turns fuzzy.

I feel my head pounding and Romeo's arm steadying me.

'Xanthe. Xanthe, what is it? What did you see?'

I'm shaking and when I touch my cheeks they're wet.

'I . . .' My thoughts are all over the place. I take the crown from my head and with trembling hands place it on the table. 'I was in Uganda again. I think it might have been the day Nani and her family had to leave. Maia was saying goodbye to Mercy – the young woman who was looking after her. She gave her this crown – I saw them take the rubies out. They were too valuable to bring. It was really sad, Romeo. Mercy said that someday Nani would come back, but she never has.'

Romeo's eyes are wide and I can see he wants to ask questions – but I blurt out one more thing, the most important thing, before he can.

'Rome, Mercy said the crown is magic, and that if Nani wore it, she would remember. Do you think, if Nani wore it now, she'd feel better?'

22

The next morning, I can't drag myself out of bed. It's like finding the crown and everything that happened last night has sent my body into a spin and sucked all my energy away.

Altogether, the memories of Nani as a girl and what happened in Uganda makes me understand how horrible it was for her. No wonder she's shut it all away.

But I know she has to accept what happened in order to heal.

Light filters through the curtains and it must be late, but still I don't get up. I allow myself to drift back to sleep, dreams of Uganda whirling through my mind, until the smell of baking and coffee tickles my nose and I blink open my eyes at last.

I hear Mum tapping on the door and check my watch. It's midday.

'Are you feeling OK?' She comes in and sits on my bed. She's brought hot milk and toast.

I push the covers away, give a yawn and take a sip of milk. 'I couldn't sleep last night.'

She strokes my cheek. 'I think I've been neglecting you, but I've been so distracted. I'm sorry.'

I rub the sleep from my eyes and think about the magic crown. 'If Nani gets better, will you stop thinking about sending her to a home?'

'Xan.' Mum clears her throat. 'This – this thing that's happening to Nani, it isn't something that's going to get better. She'll have good days and bad days and dementia is different from person to person so we just don't know.'

I bite my lip. 'But now that we're together we can help her, can't we? That's what family is about.' I tug at the duvet. 'I'm really glad we're here for her. I just don't want that to change.'

'We should do something fun together,' she says. 'We could go to Sherwood Forest, have lunch at the cafe there.'

'Sounds nice. But Mum, I've been working on something down in the basement. A surprise for Nani. I thought maybe I could show her at the weekend.'

Mum frowns.

'A really nice one. I think it might help her,' I add quickly. I don't want to tell her what it is, exactly. What if she disagrees that helping Nani remember her childhood could help her?

'Oh?' She raises her eyebrows.

'It can be a surprise for you too.'

'OK then.' She ruffles my hair and leaves me to get ready. 'You let us know when you're ready for us to see it.'

'Thanks, Mum.'

The old yellow tin with the crown in it is under my bed and it feels like I'm lying on top of a volcano. I leap from the bed, squirrel myself under it and tentatively bring out the precious tin.

I clear my desk and as carefully as I can, lift the crown on to the surface.

In the daylight I can see it all more clearly. Even without the rubies it's incredible. I blow the dust from the feathers but I know I have to take real care. Proper archaeologists would have fine brushes to do the cleaning. Maybe I can find something similar.

My fingers tremble again as I bring the crown closer, examine it properly. The band part of the crown is about the height of a small forehead and it's made up of fine gold metal, hammered out like lace leaf patterns. The feathers have been designed to make them bend in an arc shape. It's so beautiful and I imagine Mercy making it, the woman Nani loved so much she couldn't bear to leave her behind . . . She brought it all the way here to remember Mercy by, to remind her of home, but buried it when it was all too painful. I find that so sad.

I dress quickly. 'I'm going down to meet the gang,' I call, pressing the tin firmly to my chest as I hurry towards the front door.

When I get to the basement, Pria is putting finishing touches to the murals and Romeo is sweeping up the loose earth from last night.

Pria's eyes pop as soon as she looks up. 'Can I see it?' She hurries towards me. 'I can't believe there was something else buried down there, after all!'

A few weeks ago I would've been annoyed Romeo had told her – now I can't wait to prise the lid off the tin and show her what I've found.

I slide my fingers softly under the crown and lift it out.

Romeo pushes a cushion towards me and I place it gently on top.

Pria stares at it thoughtfully. 'What a strange thing to find under the tower block.'

'I know,' I agree. 'I had one of those visions again, though, to explain.' I fill her in on what I saw. 'I thought you could paint the scene to go behind the space where we place it – if there's room?'

'Totally,' says Pria. 'Look, there's the perfect gap. Maybe I could paint your nani and Mercy holding the crown?'

She's right – there's a big blank space right where our star display could go. Maybe, deep down, we were expecting to discover something else!

'When Nani sees everything we'll know whether those things actually happened or . . .' I trail off. The possibility suddenly rises up in my mind. Could all of this be one big leap of my imagination?

'Or whether Xanthe's finally given up to her dreamy side!' finishes Romeo jokingly. 'Just lightening things up,' he protests, as I gently elbow him in the side. 'So when shall we have the grand opening?' he asks, his face all lit up.

'How about Saturday, if you're both free?' I suggest. 'At eleven?'

Pria and Romeo nod.

'Afterwards we can have a celebration up in the roof garden,' I say. *Nani will be better*, I think, *and things will be like they were before*.

'That's settled then,' Romeo agrees.

Pria picks up her brush again. 'I've got a lot to do, we'd better get on.'

Saturday arrives faster than the flash of a falcon's wing. I wake early. I hope seeing the museum with all the reminders of Nani's past won't be too much for her. I hope it really will make things better.

And I hope it's not all my imagination, like Romeo said!

I can hear Dad snoring behind their bedroom door. It's going to be such a special weekend now that we're all back together as a family – except that Rajan's still away on his travels.

Mum's told Nani there's a surprise waiting for her this morning in the basement. All through the noisy breakfast I keep looking across to Nani and her eyes are sparkling with anticipation.

'I can't believe you've made this surprise just for me.'

'We've been planning it for ages.' A whirl of nerves patter through my belly. 'I really hope you like it.'

'Of course Nani will.' Dad throws an arm across my shoulders. He comes over and gives Mum a soppy kiss as he takes her empty plate and starts to clear up. 'We'll tidy up here,' he says, 'if you want to get ready for us.'

'You're such a lovely granddaughter.' Nani takes my hand. 'I can't wait to see what it is.'

'Nani's really enjoying having us around, Dad.'

'I can see that,' he grins.

'And I'm loving it too.' I squeeze Nani's hand back. 'Anyway, I'll give you a call when we're done.'

'Very mysterious,' laughs Mum. Since Dad arrived, she's more like her old self, not as touchy and tense as she has been recently.

I knock for Romeo.

'How are you feeling?' he asks, as we head down to the den.

'A bit nervy,' I confess. 'What if Nani gets upset, and all of this only makes things worse?'

'Only one way to find out.' He swings open the door to the den and we take a moment to absorb it all: everything looks incredible.

Pria strides in right behind us.

'Your paintings are amazing, Pria,' I say.

She turns pink. 'Thank you – I brought some gold paint, just to give the crown in the background the glitz it deserves.' She dips into her bag and busies herself with the final touches.

We've found long planks of wood and balanced them on some old barrels from Romeo's dad's garage to display the artefacts; they lean against the illustrations that Pria has painted.

The morning sunshine flows into the space, lighting up the murals and everything we've all worked so hard on. Loads of objects and images from Nani's past in the UK . . . and the special four items from Uganda in pride of place. The flower, the shells, the bullet bracelet and the magnificent crown.

'I can't believe we've done it,' I breathe, resting against the wall for a moment.

Pria stands back to admire her handiwork.

'Thank you.' I loop an arm around her shoulder. 'You've worked so hard to bring the visions to life – I just hope I haven't misjudged it.'

'It's coming from a good place,' she replies. 'I'm sure even if she's not ready to face her past, she'll appreciate how much you've put into this.'

A shiver of excitement tingles through my entire body.

'Ta da!' cries Romeo. 'The museum is finally ready!'

'Shall we call them?'

They both nod and we all text our parents. Even Pria's mum is coming along for the unveiling.

Pria found a wide red ribbon in her mum's sewing box and we've strung it across the entrance to the museum. 'I even sneaked out Mum's dressmaking scissors for the cutting ceremony,' she says. 'I think the staff at Wollaton would be properly impressed.'

Romeo has made a playlist and he pings it on, and suddenly we're blasted with the groovy sounds of Singo Chaka, the Ugandan singer.

We're all standing by the entrance when Nani and the rest of them timidly walk down the stairs. Romeo's mum has come, but his dad has stayed home with Mila and Evan – we didn't want to risk them knocking anything over.

'I didn't know we were coming to a disco,' says Dad, doing a silly dance.

I roll my eyes and usher them to the spot in front of the red ribbon. Now that Pearl is here, Nani introduces her properly to Mum and Dad. I feel anxious to hurry things along and as soon as the grown-ups have stopped talking I step forward.

'Isn't this out of bounds?' asks Mum, peering at

the door. 'Xanthe, I'm not sure you're technically allowed—'

'No more questions,' I say, in a hurry. 'Sorry, Mum.' Then I clear my throat. 'You've been invited here to celebrate the opening of an amazing new museum.' My voice trembles.

Mum and Dad exchange a glance, smiling now. Nani is smiling too. She's probably expecting me to show her more of my own collections. She doesn't realize that everything inside is hers. That her secrets are on display. I swallow, my throat suddenly dry. But it's too late to back out now.

'We're really proud of all the work we've done. I hope you like it. We're calling it the Tower Block Museum. As Nani's an archaeologist, I think she should cut the ribbon.'

Pria hands the scissors to Nani, who steps forward. She's still smiling, but I think she senses how nervous I am because her smile is faltering a little, like she's not sure what to expect any more.

'What an honour,' says Nani. 'Thank you, Xanthe.' She takes the scissors and makes a sharp cut through the ruby-red ribbon. 'I declare the museum officially open.'

All the grown-ups clap loudly.

'Welcome to the Tower Block Museum,' Romeo,

Pria and I shout. And then I push the door open.

Nani is the first inside.

I watch her closely to check her reactions to the displays, to make sure she's OK. She stares at the walls and at all the objects placed carefully around the room, at her name *Maia Bains*, written beautifully in the most painterly style across the top of the murals, and all her certificates pinned up.

'What do you think, Nani?' I ask gently.

She holds my hand, but doesn't say anything. It's like she's taking it all in and needs time before she can speak. I don't know if she's realized about all the stuff from Uganda yet. My stomach is all twisted up.

'That cat!' gasps Nani. 'Leo, you're here as well?'

Leo stalks the den with his head held high.

Mum frowns and shakes her head. 'There's no cat, Mum,' she whispers. Luckily, though, Mum wanders off to examine some things from Nani's schooldays.

I look over at Nani and we exchange a secretive glance. 'That's what she thinks,' I say quietly.

Nani's expression brightens.

'Wow!' Mum looks at one of the murals. 'The paintings really are spectacular. Who did these?'

'Pria,' I say proudly.

'That's wonderful, sweetheart,' says Pearl, pulling a beaming Pria in for a hug.

Then Nani's eyes fall on the case with the ruby crown in it.

'I . . . it's the magic crown,' she stutters. 'And my lucky red feather.'

'I found it, Nani,' I say gently. 'Is this OK? I want you to be able to remember. To heal.' I point out the pressed red flower, the shells and the bracelet too.

Then Nani bursts into tears and I don't know what to do.

24

I hold Nani's hand. 'I know it's a lot to take in but this is a celebration of your life. Your *whole* life. I know you didn't want to remember it for a long time, but we're here to help you through it.'

The others have gone really quiet, and Romeo's lowered the music.

Nani stares at the murals, dabbing the tears on her cheeks with her sleeve. 'How did you know about all this? I've never told anyone.'

Everyone looks in my direction but I don't want them to hear, so I whisper in Nani's ear instead. 'Nani, it was Leo that led me to the things. The first night when we came to stay, he showed me the pressed flower and when I held it in my palm, it was as if I was looking down on that moment you picked the flowers from under the flame tree. I saw it all so clearly, but I didn't understand what it meant.

The same happened with the other three things you hid.'

Nani goes over to the mural and passes her hand across the vivid colours of the paintings. 'It was Mercy who helped me,' she says. 'Always Mercy.'

I pull out a chair and help Nani sit down.

'We lived on the edge of the city in a place called Kololo,' she begins, raising her voice so everyone can hear. 'It was a large house with a beautiful garden. Papa was high up in the government . . . I remember the sound of birdsong each morning and the freshness after the rain. I loved it so much. And I loved Mercy so much too . . . it's been so long since I saw her. It was such a beautiful day on the shores of Lake Victoria, the day we collected these shells, the day my best friend Manjula told me she was leaving for Canada – I was devastated. And the bracelet . . . nothing was the same after that evening when Papa was stopped by the soldiers on our way to the airport. So many memories . . . I buried them for so long. But you're right, Xanthe – I have to accept them. The beauty comes along with the pain.'

When Nani's had lots of hugs, and she's feeling stronger, I give Romeo a signal and he puts the music back on. Everyone mills about looking at the murals and all the memories from Nani's life.

Mum hooks an arm round Nani's shoulder and plants a kiss on her cheek. 'I'm so proud of you, Mum. What an incredible life story.'

'I suppose it is,' she sighs. 'So much has happened.' She touches the crown. 'After all these years – you found it.' Morning sunshine spins across Nani's face and instead of being upset, she now looks so happy to see it. She carefully picks up the crown.

'We used to go panning for rubies up in the mountain rivers. I found quite a few and Mercy made them into a crown fit for a princess. She brought these feathers all the way from her village. Her grandfather was a tribal chief and she was so proud to show me how to make a headdress. But the crown was really special. Mercy even added my precious lucky red feather.'

It doesn't sound like Nani is confused now; it sounds like remembering her days in Uganda really is making her think more clearly.

'But what happened to the rubies?' asks Mum.

'We couldn't take anything valuable when we had to leave, so Mercy took them out. I brought this along and hid it in my case. There was hardly any room for anything else but it was so special to me – I was petrified they'd find it and that we'd be sent to a camp or something, even without the rubies.'

She shakes her head. 'It was so tough, I couldn't bear the memories. Mercy was from the Acholi tribe, you see. It wasn't only us that Idi Amin wanted rid of, it was also the people of her tribe. I don't know what would have happened to her.'

The memories fresh and full of horror flash over Nani's face. 'Once we moved to England and the tower block, I buried it all. Papa said we had to move on, get on with our new lives. I didn't feel like I could move on carrying the burden of those memories.'

Uganda is beautiful and I can understand why Nani was so upset when she left. I don't really know why we've never even visited – the country has a new president now, and new laws, so there's no reason why we shouldn't go.

Taking the crown, I place it carefully on Nani's head. There's no magic, but a peaceful expression flits over her face and she smiles. 'It fits perfectly,' I say.

'You dug it up, like a proper archaeologist,' says Dad, brushing close. 'Very impressive.'

'I'm so proud of you,' says Mum, pulling me towards her. 'All this effort for your nani – she's really touched.'

'Do we still get to celebrate on the roof garden?' asks Pria.

'Of course,' says Nani.

Once we've finished the tour Nani takes the crown off, I put it back in the tin and we all pile up to the roof garden, chattering non-stop about what's happened. Romeo's dad joins us now, with Mila and Evan rushing about in excitement.

There's food already laid out on the table and it's all covered with clean tea towels. An ice bucket full of fizzy drink cans and a couple of bottles of wine for the grown-ups sits beside it all.

We join Romeo who's brought his binoculars and is peering across the wide sky over to the other tower block.

'Can you see it?' I ask.

'Not yet.' He takes the binoculars off and hands them to me. 'Have a look.'

I hold them steady and point over to the building.

'The nest is right at the very top – there's a sort of ledge.'

'Oh yes,' I squeal. 'I see it!' The peregrine falcon is resting on the very edge of the ledge; its wings are folded and it looks like it might be watching us too. The lenses magnify his white underbelly flecked with grey, his yellow claws that grip the concrete, and I can even see his golden beak. 'Wow! That's amazing.'

I hand the binoculars back to Romeo, who passes

them round so we can all see this beautiful wild bird that's been living so close.

'They survive better in the city,' says Romeo. 'In the countryside horrible people think it's fun to shoot at them.'

Pria raises her eyebrows. 'Really? I can't imagine anyone wanting to do that. I'm going to paint the peregrine falcon. He's gorgeous.'

I think about how beautiful and unexpected things can be right next to us, even in the most ordinary of places. A falcon on the tower block roof. A magic crown buried far beneath.

I can't help feeling sorry for Nani, bringing the crown all the way with her and then burying it and having to dig down in the basement all alone. It must have broken her heart to leave it there under the dirt, but at least she can have it now and look at it and remember those hot days at the mountain streams spent panning for rubies.

Mum pours everyone a drink and we raise a toast.

'To Xanthe,' says Nani. 'And to all her friends for finding the missing crown.'

I stand up and raise my glass. 'To the bravest and most wonderful nani in the whole world.' *And to helping her heal*, I add in my head.

Everyone claps and hoots as we tuck into the fried

chicken wings and fresh garden salads.

Pearl comes over and sits beside Nani. Her face lights up like she's just had the best idea. 'One of my clients presents on Radio Notts, how about I ask if she'd like you on her show? It's not every day you find out so much history and all right under our noses.'

Nani looks a bit unsure.

'Go on, Nani.'

'I think it would be really interesting for listeners,' says Mum. 'If you're comfortable telling your story, Mum.'

I nod. 'Not many people know the Uganda story. I can help talk about what happened and you can tell everyone what it was like.'

Nani squeezes my hand. 'OK, Xanthe. I'd like that.'

Once everyone has gone, Nani, Mum, Dad and I stay on the roof, sipping drinks and discussing the museum.

Nani touches my cheek gently. 'Thank you, Xanthe, for pushing me to face it all – I didn't want to but I can already feel the stress of those years leaving me at last. The whole time I held on to the negative feelings it was like Idi Amin had won.'

'I know it was really hard but maybe now you can start to heal. I think it'll help with your other memories too.' I glance at my parents. 'I think now that she's accepted the past, Nani will get a *lot* better,' I say pointedly.

I can tell they know what I mean because they exchange this long glance. But what I'm not expecting is how their mouths are twitching . . . as if they're holding back smiles.

When she turns back to me, Mum's face is bursting with news. 'OK . . . I didn't want to say anything until we knew for sure, but . . . fingers crossed . . . we're going to move next door to Nani!'

My jaw hangs open. 'What? You mean she's not going to Treetops Lodge? But you had the leaflet and booked to visit and everything.'

'Treetops Lodge?' says Nani. 'Is that a holiday place?'

'Sort of,' says Mum. 'But we don't need to worry about that – we were trying to work things out for the best.'

Nani looks horrified as she realizes what Mum means. 'I already told you I won't go into a home.'

'And you won't,' says Mum. She clasps Nani's hand and mine. 'Didn't you hear me? We're moving in next door!'

Finally the news starts sinking in. 'So Nani doesn't have to leave the roof garden or her flat? That's awesome.' I leap up and give everyone a huge hug.

'When we found out that Patrick and Patience next door were moving we had to act fast,' Dad says.

Mum looks worried again. 'It's a big change, Xanthe, especially for you. Leaving the house you grew up in, your friends – but Dad and I can both see how much you care about Nani and want her to stay here. Enough to kidnap her!'

I giggle nervously, but everyone's smiling.

Mum goes on. 'We had to be certain the buying and selling bit would work before we mentioned it, to either of you. We didn't want to get your hopes up – and it's still not dead certain. But it looks like things might be straightforward.'

'So,' Dad takes over. 'We'll get our house on the market quickly and hope it goes smoothly. There might be hiccoughs on the way.' He crosses his fingers in the air. 'Next door have given us a bit of leeway so that's good.'

'It's the first step to a long chain of things,' says Mum.

When Mum and Dad put it like that, I suddenly understand a bit more about this complicated world they've been trying to protect me from. And when I think of our house with all its memories – the sleep-overs, the faded pencil marks on the door frame that measure each growth spurt, I do feel a pang of loss.

'You can still go to the secondary school we picked,' says Dad, guessing the thoughts racing through my mind. 'We'll drop you off at first and later you can get the bus.'

'It's just going to be different,' I say. 'People reckon everything changes once you get to secondary. You make new friends. But the great thing is I'll always have my gang here too.' I have a sudden thought. 'Actually . . . maybe I can go to the same school as them? Isn't it closer too?'

'Mmm . . .' Mum looks thoughtful. 'It's true, and Bluecoat's a great school.'

Later in bed when quiet has descended on the flat, I can't get to sleep. I turn one way then the other. I know I should be happy now, but I just can't settle.

The night is hot and sticky and I toss the covers off, flick my eyes open and go across to the window. Opening the curtains, I lift the window and let the cool night in. It's dark outside, and gentle waves of breeze wash over my bare arms. I wonder if the peregrine is sleeping on his perch over on the other tower block. If Romeo was here he'd tell me if falcons hunt at night, if they sleep with their eyes shut or whether this falcon has raised any chicks yet.

Thinking about the falcon has taken my mind off whatever was keeping me from feeling sleepy, and I close the curtains but leave the window open and slip back into bed.

Nani said I should be guardian of the ruby crown and it sits in pride of place on the shelves above my desk. I let my eyes rest on the smudgy outline of the feathers and feel my lids droop.

Drifting away into dreams of summer ending, I imagine the sharp snap of autumn and the nerves of starting a big new school, but when I think of us protecting Nani, happiness curls itself around the room and sends me into a deep sleep.

25

A few days later, Nani, Romeo, Pria and I are all sitting in the guest area at the radio station waiting to go on air.

The presenter, Polly Bruton, wears big black earphones and sits in a separate booth with hundreds of buttons on the dash which she flicks from time to time.

In front of her a fluffy microphone bobs about in the air and she leans forward to tell the listeners what's happening around the city, then pops on a happy summer track.

Romeo jumps up and starts to dance about.

Polly looks over and gives us a broad smile and suddenly her voice blares out over the speaker. 'On after this track, OK?'

I give Romeo's sleeve a yank. 'Behave,' I hiss.

The assistant shuffles everyone into the booth and

we all squish together on two chairs while Nani sits comfortably on her own seat.

'Hope you're all OK there,' says Polly. 'It's a bit tight, but it won't be for long, and just be yourselves when I introduce you in a mo.'

The track fades and Polly gives a nod before she begins to broadcast.

'Now, have you ever wondered what treasures might be buried under your house? Well, my next guests know all about archaeology and finding the most unexpected things where you'd least expect them – under a tower block.' She smiles.

'Xanthe Sharp was staying at her gran's when something extraordinary happened – what was it, Xanthe?'

I didn't expect her to ask me to speak first and my belly turns a double flip. I clear my throat. 'Um, one night while I was sleeping . . . er.'

'Go on, Xanthe,' Polly encourages me.

'A cat woke me in the middle of the night and led me downstairs to the basement.' I continue blabbing for what seems like ages and tell Polly about finding the crown and the other things.

I leave out the bits about seeing Nani's memories – and about how the cat was . . . well . . . we're not really sure! A ghost-cat, I guess? We discussed it beforehand but we think listeners won't believe it! But I do say how the objects seemed to have a kind of special resonance – and somehow I knew they were Nani's.

I don't know if it's coming out in the right order but my mouth's really dry and I wish Polly would make me stop. Instead, after I finish telling her about the museum, she thanks me and goes on to ask the others about their part in the adventure.

'Amazing!' she says, after we've finished.

'But the incredible thing,' continues Polly, 'is that this crown is out of the ordinary and tells a whole life story.' After this she brings Nani in.

'Maia Bains was born and grew up in Uganda, but in 1972 aged twelve, she was exiled from her homeland when the president Idi Amin declared that all Asian Ugandans had just ninety days to leave the country – with only fifty pounds in their pockets.' She smiles at Nani. 'But Maia smuggled something out, didn't you – what was it?'

Now it's Nani's turn to tell her side of the story. 'Thank you, Polly,' she begins.

I give Nani's hand a gentle squeeze and she explains about finding the rubies and the feathers and how she couldn't bear to leave behind the crown her closest friend, Mercy, had given her. She tells how her dreams of studying history at Makerere were never fulfilled but how she went to Cambridge and passed on her love of the subject to her grand-daughter.

A little burst of pride bubbles in my chest as I think of the way Nani has helped me find my passion.

'Now if that hasn't got you fired up to start digging, I don't know what will.' Polly finishes our chat by asking us about the end of summer and how we're feeling about going to secondary school.

'It's exciting,' says Romeo.

'I'm a bit nervous,' admits Pria. 'The school's so much bigger than my primary. And I don't know if I'll be able to do as much art when I get there – but I'm looking forward to making new friends.'

Romeo nips back into the conversation. 'I didn't get to tell you about the falcon.'

Polly frowns because it's not part of the show, but he carries on. 'I watch it every day from my window – you wouldn't expect that in the middle of the city.'

'Marvellous, and thank you all for coming in. Here's 'By Your Side' – Calvin Harris . . .'

Polly shuffles off her headphones. 'That was great, guys, thanks – you can hear it on the catch-up. Your falcon sounds impressive, Romeo. Maybe you could do a live twitching slot on the wildlife show?'

Romeo nods so furiously I think his head might roll off.

Polly gives us all a little wink. 'Jaden will show you out, and thanks again.'

Once we're back in the guest area, the assistant Jaden brings us cold drinks and a cup of tea for Nani. 'That was incredible.' He whistles. 'An actual crown all the way from Uganda!'

Now that the interview is over we can't stop chattering and letting off the nervous energy.

We thank Jaden and he leads us back to reception where Mum is waiting.

'It sounded really good,' she says, putting an arm around us and leading us to the car. 'You'll be famous now, Mum!'

'Maybe even TV next,' says Romeo, jiggling about.

We drive through the city streets with the windows down. Everyone's enjoying the last hot days of summer; people sit outside cafes wearing sunglasses and sip iced coffees or dunk their feet in the fountains in the market square.

It all whizzes by at flicker speed and now that the show's over I relax, and the buzz of being broadcast over the whole of Nottingham fills my body in a happy-go-lucky way.

Once we're home, Nani has to have a lie-down on

the sofa, but ever since she found out that we'll be moving in next door – ever since seeing her memory museum – she's been so much better and definitely less stressed.

I know Mum said that she's never going to get better completely. That there'll be good days and bad. But I feel like, with us by her side, there might just be more good days than bad.

Sliding open the window, I let the cool breeze waft in and switch on Polly Bruton's *Afternoon Show* on the catch-up.

I collapse on the armchair and together we listen to our voices echo through the sitting room.

'It doesn't even sound like us,' I say, yawning.

'I thought you did a great job,' says Nani, stretching out on the sofa.

Mum walks in from the kitchen holding her phone, a look of excitement in her eyes.

'I just had a message from Dad – we have a buyer for our house.' Mum studies me carefully. 'What do you think?'

A mix of feelings take me by surprise, and although I've been blown away about all the things Dad says he's going to do to the new flat, now that someone actually wants to buy our house it all feels so real. 'Yeah, great!' I blurt.

'It's normal to have mixed feelings,' says Mum. 'And we didn't think it would happen so quickly, but it's all good. Especially now that you're going to the same secondary school as your friends.'

It's just after lunch. Me and Nani have notebooks out on the dining table and Mum comes in jangling a set of keys.

'I managed to persuade the caretaker to let us have a look inside the flat next door. Dad and I have already seen it but I thought it would be nice for you to take a look too.'

I feel relaxed and happy that we're all going to be staying together after all. I jump up and grab Nani's hand. 'Come on.'

Mum slots the key in the lock. It's a bit sticky and she has to wiggle it a few times before it turns and the door flies open.

It's so strange seeing a home with no one living in it.

'Hi!' I call, as if it's already ours and I'm coming home from school. My voice is echoey and bounces around the bare walls.

The flat is the exact mirror of Nani's, but everything is slightly bigger. We walk into the sitting room. The paint is old and parts of it are scuffed and peeling and there's a particular smell that belongs to Patrick and Patience, Nani's old neighbours, traces that they lived here once.

'You'll soon make it homey,' says Nani, watching my face.

The sitting room has sliding doors leading on to a balcony that runs all the way along the outside of the flat. Mum pushes them open and we pile out. Dried-out plant pots and empty sweet wrappers pepper the concrete slabs.

I fix my eye on the tower block opposite, growing into the sky like a giant with hundreds of gaping mouths, and find the spot Romeo showed us, where the peregrine nests. I'm not sure if I can see him or not but I imagine him there perched on the edge of the building, ready to take flight and soar between the clouds towards me.

'We can put plants and things here,' says Mum, peering round the corner. 'Because it's the end flat the far bedroom has windows on two sides. Let's take a look.'

We go back in and walk down the narrow corridor that goes off the hallway and leads to the bedrooms. All the doors are open and yellow sunlight washes over the old swirly carpets.

Mum walks past the first two bedrooms and leads

us into the final one. It's full of light that spins into the dusty nooks of the room.

'This could be yours.'

The windows join at the corner so the sky fills the entire space.

'It'll be like sleeping in the clouds,' says Nani.

'And Dad's already been planning how he's going to change things to make it extra special. We're going to turn the middle bedroom into another bathroom, so you can have your own.'

'What about Rajan? Where will he sleep when he comes back from his travels?'

'We thought it would be nice if he had a room on my side,' says Nani. 'Walking through here reminds me of the first time we stepped into our flat all those years ago.' Nani gets a distant look in her eye like she does when she thinks of the past. 'And even though Papa worked in the government in Uganda, when he applied to the civil service here, they said his qualifications weren't quite right.'

'I know it was a disappointment for him.' Mum moves closer to Nani. 'He had to start back down the ladder but he soon worked his way up again.'

'That's true. He was such a hard worker. It's amazing what you can do if you focus and don't give up.'

We pull the door closed and go back to Nani's flat, which suddenly looks like it's got too much stuff in it.

Mum pours me a drink and gives me a quizzing look. 'Well?'

'I think once we've got the carpet out and done the fancy stuff Dad's planning, it'll be a totally different place. And I did really love all the sky windows in my room. I'll be able to lie in bed and watch the peregrine.' I meet Mum's eyes. 'Basically, I think it's awesome.'

We spend days furiously whizzing between the house and the flat, packing everything up. It's woken all the memories from when I was little and makes me understand just a bit of what Nani went through when she was moved thousands of miles from her home.

I've brought my favourite cuddlies and they're lined up on my bed now. I know I'm too old for them, but I can't seem to give them up.

One morning we're all squeezed around Nani's kitchen table having breakfast.

'What do you think about taking a big family trip this year?' says Dad. 'I thought we could visit Uganda.'

26

The long summer holidays have been over for weeks, but instead of getting cooler the sun begins to beat from the skies, crisping the grass and sending us up to the roof garden to soak in its rays. The nights are clammy hot and we sleep with the windows open, soft wind whistling the curtains.

We've all started at our new school and being with Romeo and Pria has made all the changes so much easier. We're in different tutor groups but get together every break time.

Rajan is back from his travels and now that the house is properly sold all our belongings are in storage, except for a couple of boxes of important stuff, and we're all squished in Nani's flat.

Months pass as the builders knock down walls, install new bathrooms and put in cool sliding doors.

We're connecting the two flats. Dad calls it *broken living* – that's architect-speak for being able to open up spaces when you want to be airy and close in when you need to be cosy.

Nani says the banging is driving her to distraction, but I know she's only joking, because even with all the chaos she's better than ever. It's not that the dementia has gone away but things have slowed and most importantly, there's always someone around.

Finally the new build is finished and Friday night is here. We're throwing a house-warming party. It's the Christmas holidays and we've put up all the decorations. Dad's laid out a table with drinks, music is blasting through the speakers in the ceilings and the space is dotted with flickering tea lights. The orange blush of the late afternoon sun is dipping behind the clouds and the glow washes through the open doors, turning everything a beautiful gold.

Rajan and Nani are chatting on the balcony.

The doorbell rings and the first guests come in.

'Wow!' It's Romeo's parents. They got a baby-sitter for tonight so they could come to the party.

'Are we in New York?' jokes his dad. 'You've done an incredible job.'

'You wouldn't think it was two separate flats not

long ago,' says his mum, eyeing up the cool furniture. 'It's so spacious.'

I pull Romeo aside. 'I'll get you a drink, what do you want?' We walk over to the table and I pour him a glass of iced tea. 'How was school today?' I ask, sipping my juice. 'I didn't catch you at lunch.'

'Good – sorry I missed you, I spent lunch in the music studio, practising for our big concert. What about you?'

'Good. It's been chaos at home with all of this going on.' I nod at the air. 'School's been a bit of a sanctuary.'

The bell rings again and more guests arrive – neighbours, Pria with her parents, and people from Mum's and Dad's jobs who I don't recognize.

'Pria – over here!' The music's even louder now and I have to raise my voice over the noise of the chatter.

I ask her what she'd like, then hand her a Coke. 'How are things with your parents now?' I ask carefully. I peer over at her mum and dad – I've not seen them together before. They look happy.

'Much better since they went for counselling,' she says. 'Thanks for asking. They're giving it another try, so fingers crossed.' She looks around. 'This is proper posh,' she says. 'I can't even believe it's the same flat.'

'I know – Dad's gone for gold.'

'When's your trip to Uganda?' asks Romeo. 'Must be coming up.'

'Next week! We're going to spend Christmas out there, I'm so excited.'

'That will be nice for your nani,' says Pria.

'I know – going back for the first time. And it's mine and Mum's heritage too. It'll be so interesting seeing things for the first time in real life. Although the feelings were so strong each time I saw the places in the visions, there are still things that aren't fully explained, like what happened to Mercy or the rubies.'

We walk through the buzzing open-plan sitting room towards my bedroom. 'I've got something special to show you.' I slide the door open and we all step inside.

Pria eyes the bathroom. 'Nice!'

'I have to squeeze in with the whole family,' cries Romeo.

'I didn't have my own in the other house. I think Dad planned a few treats for us, just so the whole space will last us into the future.'

'It must make you feel really proud that your family have lived here for so long,' says Romeo.

'Nani is one of the longest residents and Mum

211

grew up here too,' I say, as I lead them to my sky window. 'It's all about community, that's what Nani says.'

Dad's replaced the window to one side with a floor-to-ceiling glass door and I push it open. Outside, the night has swallowed up the sunset and tiny stars are glimmering way above us.

I stand at the edge of the balcony, the others right beside me. 'The *really* cool thing is that we're right opposite Romeo's falcon, and when he goes hunting I've seen him shoot through the night like a star.'

Romeo smiles and we stay there together at the edge of the world, staring up at the stars and the deep dark sky. I imagine us all doing amazing things in the future: Romeo the musician, Pria the artist and me an archaeologist. It makes me happy.

'What Dad's done with the flats and everything is great, but the real magic is all this.' We hook arms.

'To friends.'

'And to more summers of adventures.'

27

Ten days later, I run barefoot from the Hotel Kampala steps, across the grass still damp with early morning dew and into the lush gardens, where Nani is sitting under a flame tree, its copper-red leaves dancing above her. The air is filled with the sound of exotic birdsong and a warm breeze wraps me in rich flower scents.

Joining Nani under the shimmering tree, I pull out a chair and dig my spoon into the blush-orange papaya arranged beautifully on the platter before me. It's soft and fragrant, sweet and delicious, and slips down my throat like nothing I've ever tasted before.

'What do you think?' asks Nani. 'Do you like it?'

'I wish I could have papaya for breakfast every day.'

'I can't believe I'm here.' Nani stares up through the red leaves, their shadow patterns moving over her face. 'After all this time.'

'We're going to do a tour today – we can go wherever you want, you're in charge.'

She smiles. 'I never thought I'd come back, too many things I didn't want to remember, but it makes me so happy to see it all now and to know it's still here and just as beautiful.' She touches her chest. 'It's making my heart sing and I can't wait to visit all my favourite places.'

The waiter dressed in a starched white outfit brings us warm pastries and tea for Nani, and a pineapple smoothie for me.

'Thank you.'

'I think it's going to be another wonderful day,' he says, putting the tray on the table. 'A good day for a trip to Lake Victoria maybe? To see the marabou storks?'

'Can we, Nani?'

'Is it still as wonderful?' asks Nani. 'I went there as a girl, took picnics and boat rides with my friends.'

The waiter crinkles his eyes at Nani. 'It's still as beautiful, stretching way away, deepest blue like a precious inland sea.'

'Boat rides!' I'm getting really excited now. 'Can we, *please*?'

'Well, have fun whatever you decide,' he says, straightening the tablecloth, before returning inside.

Mum, Dad and Rajan appear from between the tall flapping palms.

'Hey, lazybones,' I call as they come and sit with us for breakfast.

Rajan yawns and pushes his hand through his dark curly hair. 'I slept so well, I didn't want to get up.'

'But then you'd miss all this – and we might go to Lake Victoria today. There are boat rides and everything!'

'Someone's excited,' says Mum, giving me a kiss.

'Isn't this just incredible?' says Dad, sitting down and pouring himself a coffee from the shiny cafetiere.

'I feel like I already know Uganda,' says Mum, looking across at Nani. 'Seeing it for the first time with my own eyes, I know why leaving was so hard.'

'But it's all still here,' says Nani. 'In all its wonder – and I can't wait to see everything again.'

After breakfast we get into the hire car and drive out of the swanky hotel into the buzzing streets of Kampala, Uganda's capital city. It's busy with traffic and people on scooters and bikes weave in and out of the lanes. Skyscrapers stretch high into the blue skies and in the distance the wooded hills of Kololo where Nani lived hang like a soft green cloud over the city.

I wind the window down and let the morning sun

warm my face; all the noises of this city that Nani loves so much wash over me: sounds of beeping horns, the hum of traffic and faint voices of people going about their day on the pavements that snake alongside the road.

We leave the busier roads behind and instead of taking the sign for Lake Victoria, Dad turns to a quieter road marked *Kololo*.

A snap of disappointment catches me out as I realize we're not going on a boat ride today, but are headed to where Nani used to live.

We drive through an area of Kampala where the houses are squat blocks of concrete painted rust red, the same colour as the earth. They are surrounded by gardens planted with all sorts of vegetables.

'Xanthe, look!' says Nani, pointing at a roof.

'It's like a mini version of our roof garden,' I laugh. The roof of the house has a metal trough attached to it and it's brimming with sweetcorn and bright yellow squash.

'What a great idea,' says Rajan. 'Sustainable living in action.'

Kololo has wider roads and houses set back in large gardens; the sweet sound of birdsong peppers the air and I point my phone into the trees to try and get photos, but all I manage to capture are blurred green leaf shapes.

Dad glances at the satnav which takes us down a windy narrow road and opens up to a group of houses that branch off either side.

Nani takes a deep breath. 'This is it. Our family home.'

We park outside a red-brick two-storey house with a neatly trimmed lawn and tall swaying palms in front. It has stone pillars and a verandah that runs along the outside. It's the same place I saw in my visions and I feel a tingle creep up my spine.

'Do you think they'll mind us coming?' Nani's looking a bit unsure.

'We can only be polite and ask,' says Mum. 'They might say no, but then again they might say yes.'

We walk into the garden towards the front door, where a woman is sweeping leaves away from the drive, the sounds of children playing further off in the garden behind the house rising towards us.

'Mercy?' Nani calls out, her voice wavering.

The woman is young and slender and wears a long printed dress, her hair swept up in a matching headscarf.

'May I help you?'

'I'm sorry,' says Nani. 'I – I thought you were my Mercy.'

The young woman clears her throat. 'I'm Dembe,' she says, looking confused.

'I lived here years ago and Mercy looked after me when I was a girl.' She wipes her cheek. 'I loved her.'

An older woman appears on the verandah; she's wearing a brightly coloured scarf and leans on a walking stick. Her back is slightly bent and she shuffles along. 'Who is it, Dembe?'

'We're sorry to disturb you but we're over from England,' says Dad, walking closer to the house while we all stay where we are. 'My mother-in-law used to live here a long time ago. She just wanted to see it again. I hope you don't mind?'

We're not very close so I can't see if the woman is happy about us visiting or not. I see Dad handing her the gift we brought – a snow globe of Big Ben – and talking to her as if he's trying to explain things.

28

The older woman waves us over in a friendly way. She squints towards us, and suddenly her expression changes and she hurries towards Nani and they both clasp each other tightly.

'Maia,' she cries, holding Nani's face. Tears track down both their cheeks.

'Mercy.' Nani repeats her name over and over.

When there are no more tears left Mercy seems to notice that we're all still standing in the garden.

'This is my granddaughter Dembe. And this' – she hugs Nani even more tightly – 'is my dearest Maia come back to me like we promised.'

I remember the moment when Mercy was wrapping the rubies in the cloth and how hard it was and how she promised they'd find each other again once it was all over. I bet she didn't think they'd have to wait this long.

'I'll get some tea.' Dembe disappears into the house.

'Come, come,' says Mercy, ushering us to the armchairs.

Dembe returns with a tea tray, and three children who shyly tag along behind her as she places the tray on the low table in front of the chairs.

'Say hello nicely to Great-grandmamie's friends,' says Dembe.

The three small children look so alike and they say hello politely before running back off into the trees to play.

Nani and Mercy don't stop talking and laughing and holding hands.

Nani stares into the house through the open door. Mercy springs up and leads her towards it. 'After you left, things got very bad here. So much fighting. Even though, as you know, Amin was no friend of the Acholi, we held our ground and we were allowed to stay here, in the family house.'

Nani nods and seems so happy that Mercy didn't lose her home.

'Come see inside,' she says, leading us into the house. 'Still the same after all these years. We hoped you'd come back with your mama and papa.'

Nani smiles and I see a side to her I've never

noticed. She seems more confident suddenly and I can see that this is what it means to come home at last.

It's dark inside after the brightness of the sun in the garden and I have to blink so I can see properly.

There's a big sitting room with an archway to one side. 'That's my desk,' says Nani, lighting up. 'I'd do my homework sitting here, looking out over the garden.'

We climb the sweeping staircase that I've seen before, each step strangely familiar.

'Your room,' says Mercy, opening the dark wooden door. Inside, the walls are painted brightly with patterns in reds and blues. There are three small beds next to each other with neatly folded pyjamas on the pillows and a cuddly toy on top.

'It looks a bit different now,' smiles Nani. 'But it's so lovely the children have it.' She walks to the window. 'I used to listen to the owls hooting at night from here.'

When we come back downstairs Dembe has laid the table with food.

'You'll stay for lunch?' asks Mercy. 'There's all your favourites – gonja, muchomo and even the sweet mandazi you loved so much.'

'Of course we'll stay for lunch.' Nani is laughing now and she's so completely at home. 'It's just like old times! Remember, Mercy, all the laughter and life, friends coming and going?'

'Your papa used to have colleagues over for cock-tails on the verandah.'

They both heave a long sigh and we heap our plates with the wonderful Ugandan feast.

We're just getting up to leave when something brushes my leg. I look down and over to Nani. She saw it too!

Then Mercy catches both our eyes. 'Leo?' she mouths at Nani.

She's right: it is Leo! I haven't seen the ghost-cat since he appeared at the museum opening. I thought that was his way of saying goodbye.

But does he have something else to show us, after all?

'What are you three staring at?' asks Mum. She looks right where Leo is sitting, but her eyes seem to gloss over him.

'Come on,' I say, ignoring Mum, and together Nani, Mercy and I follow the cat that only the three of us seem to be able to see. He leads us through the jungle of the garden, along the spiral of paths that wind their way between borders crammed with roses until we're under the flame tree, the tree where Nani picked the pressed flower.

Everyone has gathered beneath it and Leo pounces on the base and begins to scratch. 'Do you have a spade, please?' I ask Dembe, who looks a little unsure but runs off to get one.

'Leo,' says Nani, bending down to coax the cat closer. He stands his ground, but purrs loudly. 'It *is* you, isn't it? He was always such a mischievous rascal.'

Rajan edges closer and crinkles his brow at the very spot where the cat is standing. The others peer over my shoulder as Leo makes a long mewl and rubs his back against the bark of the tree.

'I just don't get what you're looking at,' says Rajan.

And I think how only Nani, Mercy and I share the memories of their childhood. Maybe that's why the ghost of Leo exists only for us.

As soon as Dembe returns with the spade I dig into the hard soil.

'Just wait,' I say, pushing my weight against the spade. 'He always leads me to hidden things.'

It takes a while to shift the soil, but after all the practice with the digging under the tower block, my muscles are toughening up. Dembe's children think it's a great game and they help too, with their own toy spades. Together, we begin to make progress.

'Is it OK to dig your garden up?' asks Mum, looking apologetically at Dembe.

'If Granny thinks it's OK,' she laughs, 'I guess it's OK.'

After a while of digging, something different emerges from the earth and I fall to my knees, now pulling the soil away with my hands in case we damage anything.

Nani and Mercy move closer as I lift a package wrapped in layers of muddied old newspaper.

Mercy blinks as I show her what the cat has found. Even though I didn't see this part in my vision, I feel as though I'm finally coming to the end of the story.

I hand the package to Mercy and she takes it with open palms.

'I remember . . .' she says softly.

She lays it under the flame tree and together Nani and Mercy carefully pull back the wads of yellowed newspaper.

Everyone crowds round now, a look of shock plastered to their faces at the glimmering red light emerging from the package as Nani unfolds the final layer. Even Rajan is wide-eyed.

'I hid the rubies in your old bedroom,' whispers Mercy. 'The soldier patrols were rounding people up, ransacking homes, taking anything they could. But when I returned for the rubies, they were gone. I thought they'd been taken by the soldiers . . . but someone must've buried them. To keep them safe.'

My gaze lifts to Leo, sitting on the edge of the woodland with his bright eyes and swishing tail. 'He's actually quite good at digging,' I whisper thoughtfully, remembering how he had helped me uncover the shells.

Nani reaches out for the rubies. They've been protected well over all the years; even the cloth is not too worn. The red gems shine in the afternoon light, the crimson flowers of the flame tree perfect against their fire.

I look up to find Leo again, to thank him, but of course he's disappeared. And this time, I know in my heart it's for good.

'Ten precious rubies,' breathes Mercy, 'taken from the magical ruby crown.' She holds them up to the sunlight. 'And now you can put them back and make it fit for a princess again.'

Nani shakes her head. 'No, Mercy, these are for you. Use them for your family. Maybe it will help them to go to Makerere University like I wanted to, once.'

Mercy doesn't agree straight away but after Nani

insists that the rubies should stay with her family, she wraps Nani in a warm hug. They agree never to lose touch again now they have found each other at long last.

Our last day in Uganda arrives too quickly and we finally make our trip to Lake Victoria. We're all squished together at the front of the boat, the water lapping against the sides. The lake is a vast mirror of blue, like being at sea. The waves, even though the day is calm, are curling up and splashing high in the air.

I remember Nani finding the shells, most likely on the beach over there. It's so strange how one thing leads to another. The ghost-cat, the objects and the memories that now feel so real it's as if I was the one collecting the shells and making the ruby crown. I imagine a chain of memories and objects stretching back to me, Mum, Nani, to her parents and grandparents and all the way back through time.

Mum and Dad throw their arms around our shoulders.

'Thank you for this,' says Nani. 'I know how hard it's been to work it all out.'

'Life's an adventure,' says Rajan. 'That's what my travelling year taught me.'

We watch the beauty of Uganda unfurl before us in all its vivid colours, sparkles of water like sequins on a sari and the echoing voices of laughter, friendship and family.

LETTER FROM THE AUTHOR

When I began thinking about writing my fourth novel, I knew I wanted to set this one much closer to home than my other stories.

I grew up in Nottingham and, with my brothers and sisters, had the most wonderful adventures in the city. We would play around the tower blocks, walk to Wollaton Park with our dog Sabre, and during the long hot summers we'd always find fun ways to entertain ourselves. Although we never dug down into a basement, it's just the sort of thing that would have filled us with enthusiasm. We were always on the lookout for something unusual or magical.

One of the other things I wanted to do in this

story was to shine a light on an aspect of Indian history that is often overlooked – the expulsion in 1972 of many thousands of Asian people from Uganda, Africa, by the then-president Idi Amin.

As a girl I recall family friends suddenly having close relatives join them. One grandfather in particular stayed in my memory – he was strikingly tall, smart and educated. At the time I didn't understand why he had to leave his home.

I did a lot of research into what happened and watched BBC news reports to find out what impact this announcement had on ordinary people. Reading the wonderfully vivid novel *Kololo Hill* by Neema Shah helped me to build an authentic back story for Xanthe's nani, as well as giving me all the sights and sounds for this beautiful country.

As is the case with these things, the background to this moment in history is complex. In the late 1800s Britain made Uganda a British Protectorate and it became part of the Commonwealth. Since India was already part of the British Empire, people were sent to Uganda to work.

So by 1972 Ugandan Asians had been part of the country for many many years and Uganda was their home. They owned businesses, worked in government and taught in the schools and at the university.

Idi Amin was the chief of the army and air force and came to power in 1971 through a coup d'état while the then-president Milton Obote was out of the country. On 4 August 1972 Amin gave the order that all the Asian Ugandans had ninety days to leave the country.

They were not allowed to take any belongings with them apart from £50.

It was a time of huge hardship, turmoil and chaos. Since the large majority of the population had British passports, the British Government – led by Prime Minister Edward Heath – offered sanctuary.

I began wondering how it would feel if you were a young girl, as Xanthe's nani was in 1972, and you had to leave everything you had ever known. When we bury traumatic memories they have to surface sometime. In this book I wanted to bring those memories out of the shadows and give them a magical twist to allow Nani to come to terms with what happened.

I so enjoyed building the setting of the tower block roof garden that Nani's papa created when he arrived from Uganda. For me it represents how we can transform our environment, that everywhere we live there are incredible things just waiting to be uncovered.

This book is about identity, belonging and coming to terms with our past, so we can be more resilient and live a hopeful and brilliant future.

ACKNOWLEDGEMENTS

I can't quite believe that this is my fourth book. Each time I begin the first musings for a story I'm unsure where I'll end up. But one thing is clear – it's the faith and support of so many people that has made *Xanthe & the Ruby Crown* a reality.

Firstly huge thanks to my family: Ian, Gem and Satchen, my mum and my siblings Balraj, Sherry, Randhiraj, Dip and Amolack. To my nieces and nephews Avarni, Jyodh, Arran, Ashari, Rajan, Xanthe, Thara, Rubuen, Rani, Evan, Jaden, Arron, Aneve, Josh and Kiran.

To the magnificent Team Chicken House who pulled out the stops, as always, to create an actual book from my scribblings. Special thanks to Kesia, my editor, who is always right about EVERY-THING! Jazz, Sarah, Laura, Liv, Esther, Elinor and Emily. To Barry for saying yes to more stories, Rachel L for whipping up some extra magic and slipping it in just where it was needed, and to Rachel H for creating another stunning cover to go with the other three. When I see them side by side my heart begins to sing! To Bex Parkin and Steve Wells for the glorious artwork.

Michelle was my best friend all through secondary school where we shared so much laughter – thank you for your deep friendship.

Miranda and Mel are my trusty second eyes. They have been so generous with their time and for this I am forever grateful. I know I have to pay in champagne but I wouldn't have it any other way.

Thank you to Mrs Manjula Datta, who gave up precious time to talk about her idyllic childhood growing up in East Africa and shared her wonderful memories.

Hyon-mi McAlpine grew up in Uganda and generously agreed to do a very early historical read. Her comments that the book gave an authentic and touching portrayal meant so much.

To Ben Illis for all his enthusiasm and support.

I'm so proud to be a Nottingham girl. Thank you

to Mellers School – my Patron of Reading School and my own incredible primary – for all the cheering and for naming your new library after me. Wow! Mellers is the best school ever! It's where the seeds of my creativity were sown, and look what we did!

It means so much to have the support and encouragement of Nottingham City of Literature, Read on Nottingham and The Literacy Trust.

To the teachers and librarians who work tirelessly to bring magic and stories to all children, you are true heroes.

Finally to you, dear reader – thank you for picking up this book and having faith in my stories. Let the magic begin!